FIGHTING THE DYING LIGHT

TEN STORIES OF AGING

DAVID H. HENDRICKSON

PP
Pen-&-Ink
Publishing

Willard sits at the head table, his crimson bowtie tight against his neck, his white shirt uncomfortably tight, and his black suit jacket snug in the shoulders. Beside him, Edna looks like Zsa Zsa Gabor, dressed to the nines in her nicest dark blue party dress, long dangling earrings, sparkling necklace, and her hair made up fancy thanks to three hours at the beauty salon. Even as the lingering smells of baked chicken, tomato sauce, and red wine fill the air, a three-layer cake with white icing and a basketball-sized gold decoration with "90" in the middle is wheeled out in front of him on the other side of the fifty-foot long head table.

The Knights of Columbus hall is filled with rows of circular tables, six people to each, radiating out from an open, wooden dance floor. The hall buzzes with loud conversation and peals of laughter. Edna tells him these are all friends and relatives, almost two hundred in all, some of whom flew cross country just for the celebration.

But they all look like strangers to Willard. He can't find a face he recognizes.

PRAISE FOR DAVID H. HENDRICKSON

Fighting the Dying Light, Ten Stories of Aging

"End of the Line," originally appeared in *Fiction River Special Edition: Spies*, edited by Kristine Kathryn Rusch, WMG Publishing, Inc., March, 2019

"*Makonde* Tree of Life," originally appeared in *Fiction River Special Edition: Editor Saves*, edited by Kristine Kathryn Rusch, WMG Publishing, Inc., August, 2018

"The Amazing RBG," originally appeared in *Pulphouse Fiction Magazine*, Issue #11, edited by Dean Wesley Smith, WMG Publishing, Inc., April, 2021

"One-Night Stands for Love and Glory" originally appeared in *Fiction River: Universe Between*, edited by Dean Wesley Smith, WMG Publishing, August, 2014

"Sully and the Geezer," originally appeared in *Mystery, Crime, and Mayhem: The Chase Begins*, edited by Leah Cutter, Knotted Row Press, August, 2020

"Only One Remains," originally appeared in *Mystery, Crime, and Mayhem: Blood on the Tracks*, edited by Leah Cutter, Knotted Row Press, May, 2023

"Role of a Lifetime," originally appeared in *Pulphouse Fiction Magazine*, Issue #10, edited by Dean Wesley Smith, WMG Publishing, Inc., February, 2021

"Truth and Lies" originally appeared in *Fiction River: Feel the Love*, edited by Mark Leslie, WMG Publishing, February, 2019

This is a work of fiction. Names, characters, places, and events are either the product of the author's imagination or are used fictitiously, and any resemblance to actual persons, living or dead, business establishments, events, or locales is entirely coincidental.

ISBN-13: 978-1-948134-18-7

CONTENTS

To Mom,
In life, you taught me how to live.
In death, you taught me how to fight the dying light.
You will always live on in my heart.

INTRODUCTION

Almost all my stories are personal to me in one way or another. A writer cannibalizes his life in bits and pieces, sometimes in flagrant fashion but most often in tiny fragments without even realizing it. My characters are mine alone, born out of my experiences. My voice is mine alone. There may be countless similarities to countless stories by countless other writers, but somewhere in a David H. Hendrickson story is something that is mine and mine alone.

Especially these stories.

The smart alecks in the peanut gallery will point out that I'm hardly a spring chicken so of course a themed collection based on advancing age will be deeply personal. Geezer Hendrickson ain't revealing anything surprising there.

Admittedly, there's an element of truth to that. I'm at an age where concerns about aging have become *Holy crap! Concerns about aging!* Or perhaps more accurately, *Mayday! Mayday! Mayday! Concerns about aging!*

I'll plead guilty to that charge.

But there's also the matter of my mother. My father died at the age of sixty-five, before he could enjoy the pleasures of old age and battle its problems. Not so my mom.

Mom passed away on April 7, 2022, at the age of ninety-three. She was a sweet, loving woman whose kindness belied the abuse she endured as a child. I loved her dearly.

In her last few years, she suffered many of the afflictions of old age, both of the mind and body. In particular, dementia increasingly robbed her of some of life's pleasures and occasionally plunged her back into the horrors of her abusive childhood. One time, I had to take her hand while sitting with her at her kitchen table, tears filling her eyes, and assure her that no, she did not have to leave that very instant because she would be punished by her stepmother or father for getting home late. She *was* home. And her parents were long-since dead and could never hurt her again.

But aside from the rare need to occasionally reset her back to present-day reality, she would be smiling and alert for our weekly dinners, dressed to the nines, fighting the good fight to hold onto as much of her mental faculties as possible. I admired that fight almost as much as I felt *supreme* admiration and gratitude that she did not perpetuate the cycle of abuse that she had experienced. It stopped with the brick wall of her love.

Before health and safety concerns prompted her to move into a beautiful retirement home, we would meet for breakfast every week. After the move, that tradition became dinner, either going out to a restaurant or staying in at the quite elegant restaurant within her facility. After the pandemic hit, I brought dinner to her apartment and we'd eat there.

After dinner, we'd "co-write" a page-long entry in her journal, a notebook born out of her memory loss issues. It recorded her events of the day so caregivers could read them back to her, reminding her of pleasant visits and events she had already forgotten. I did the writing in that journal, but she was the boss. The number one rule was that I could never say anything bad about myself. Not with her as the "lead co-writer." Even if it was funny and I argued for its inclusion, she would relent only if it was extraordinarily funny and I argued really hard. Anything that funny, I claimed, would make for more enjoyment later when caregivers read the entry back to her.

After her death, there was no question which of us four sons would get those journals. They would be mine and mine alone.

Those dinners were great times and always a priority. Even with a day job and sometimes teaching an additional three nights a week, "Dinner with Mom" was always a non-negotiable, weekly blessing for both of us.

All but one of the stories in this collection were written during that time and thus were heavily influenced, if not outright inspired, by those wonderful evenings. Many of the stories are set in a retirement home, some with the general layout of my mom's apartment. A large number of them involve the struggle to hold onto one's mental faculties even as advanced age tries to steal them away. This collection has my mom and our times together written all over it.

Small wonder this book is dedicated to her. I will always remember and love her. As the plaque I once gave her reads, "It was from you, that I learned to be me." To which I added, "The bad parts about me are my fault."

Love you, Mom.

All that said, none of these characters are representations of my mother. None. Not even close. Not even the one affectionately referred to as "Mrs. H" by a caregiver even though that was a name many who loved my mother used for her. Please don't try to read her into any of these characters. Mom was not a spy, never visited Africa, and never became convinced she was a Supreme Court justice.

One last heads up. The good guy doesn't always win in these stories. In the battle with aging and death, the best one can do is fight the good fight against the dying light, as my mom did, for as long as one can.

Carpe diem.

—May 18, 2024

END OF THE LINE

INTRODUCTION TO "END OF THE LINE"

*F*iction River, where this story first appeared, is my kind of anthology series. Although each issue is themed, the genre varies from mystery to suspense to romance to science fiction to fantasy to pure thriller to mainstream to who-knows-what and everything in between.

All over the map. Kind of like yours truly. Kind of like this collection.

It's been my privilege to appear in ten *Fiction River* volumes with eleven of my stories. I hope to appear in more in the future. *Fiction River* went on hiatus during the pandemic but is in the process of resuming publication. That's great news. It gives readers a chance to read more stories like "End of the Line." A wonderful thing about theme-based anthologies, you see, is that they prompt writers to write stories they otherwise wouldn't have even considered.

I wrote this one for a special *Fiction River* spies-themed issue. I had no plans at that time of writing any spy story at all and had no ideas lurking in my folders. If no *Fiction River: Spies*, then no "End of the Line."

And if my thoughts hadn't also so often been focused on my mother and aging, then I'd have written something completely different. No "End of the Line." In fact, the dinner spent by the story's two lead characters is modeled directly after many of those I enjoyed with my mother.

So if you like this story, send a good thought my mom's way. If you don't like it, blame me.

END OF THE LINE

All Ferguson had been getting was shit assignments. It had been that way for years. Shit, followed by crap, then finally crapola. And when that was done, Gallagher assigned him shit all over again to restart the cycle. Ferguson could barely remember his last prime assignment, one that had actually made him work at it a little, and not just go through the motions.

He didn't complain. Who was he going to complain to? And who, after listening, would be able to do anything about it? When it came to The Unit, Gallagher answered to no one, and it had been that way for over thirty years, so no one was foolish enough to complain to him. So each time Gallagher dropped a new load of shit on him, Ferguson kept his mouth shut and grabbed a shovel.

This assignment, however, was a new low. Lower than shit, crap, and crapola. Not just beneath him, but beneath him all the way down to the center of the Earth.

An insult to his intelligence, to his abilities, to his decades in The Unit.

Only one way he'd have to work at all on this one.

SAL SAVIANO'S handshake practically broke half the bones in Ferguson's hand. The old man had just turned eighty-one and had lived in the posh retirement home known as Golden Vistas for almost a decade, but he still had his fastball. Still the same distinguished, lawyer-like, thick white hair, the same cinnamon-scented cologne, and the same barrel-shaped chest and thick, powerful forearms that made any handshake with him just another form of hand wrestling. Impeccably dressed, as always, he wore a tailored beige sports jacket over a crisp blue shirt that made Ferguson's unbuttoned winter coat and beneath it, the shiny, black sports jacket and white shirt look shabby by comparison.

Plastic surgery had smoothed out most of Saviano's facial wrinkles, making him look even younger than Ferguson, who was twenty years his junior. And though Saviano needed a walker, he'd blasted out of his apartment without even inviting Ferguson inside, and now was racing double-time with that black-and-maroon walker of his down the hallway, two steps ahead of Ferguson, as if he'd planted a bomb back in his own apartment and they'd better clear the area before it went off.

"You look fabulous, Sal," Ferguson said, quickening his stride to keep up as they streaked past one apartment door after another, each adjacent wall decorated in some unique way: flowers, framed art, and especially, pictures of grand-kids and great-grandkids. "I'll bet you're popular with the ladies, just like in the old days. Comforting the widows every afternoon?"

"How you think I broke my hip?" Saviano said, and they both guffawed. The broken hip had necessitated the walker, according to the reports, but otherwise didn't seem to have slowed the old man down.

They stepped onto the elevator, and Saviano pressed the button for the second floor, which, in addition to more apartments, housed the nicest of the five restaurants in the facility, at least according to the reports. This was Ferguson's first visit.

"Are you sure you don't want to go out to eat?" Ferguson asked. "Legal Seafoods. Magianno's. Ruth's Chris for a thick, juicy steak. You name it. Get some fresh air. Get out of this place for a few hours."

"It's thirteen degrees out there," Saviano said, as the elevator door opened. "Down to three or four with the wind chill. I have no interest in freezing my nuts off. If you do, be my guest and I'll meet you back at the apartment in a couple hours."

Ferguson declined.

"Besides, it's near the end of the month, and I haven't used all the meals on my plan. Use 'em or lose 'em. So it's free. And the food's good."

Saviano had always been frugal, Ferguson recalled. Probably why he could afford this most luxurious of retirement homes. He'd also been the best at what they did. A legend. And there had been, no doubt, opportunities on the side.

They stepped off the elevator and Saviano raced off with his walker, once again leaving Ferguson in his wake to hustle and catch up. Saviano passed other residents going the same way like a new, red Ferrari zooming past rusted-out Hyundais, nodding and smiling and waving as he did but never slowing down. Residents walking in the other direction all flashed him warm smiles and the occasional greeting. By the time they reached the restaurant several hundred yards from the elevator, Ferguson's awe for the old man had only increased.

This whole assignment was a waste of time.

Saviano put his name in with the *maître d*, a pretty, dark-haired young woman barely out of high school, and took a buzzer in return. They retired to a side waiting room filled on one side with twenty or so rectangular tables, mostly empty except for men and women playing bridge in one corner and two men played chess in the other. On the other side, a dozen dark brown leather lounge chairs formed a half circle around a blazing fireplace. Saviano ordered them both a glass of Cabernet from a tuxedoed Latin young man, and they settled into a pair of the middle lounge chairs, three chairs away from the nearest resident.

Following Saviano's lead, Ferguson sniffed the wine, then sipped it. It was *good*, far better than the cheap stuff he could afford.

"You've done well," Ferguson said, gesturing to their surroundings as a log in the fireplace snapped.

Saviano smiled. "I'm comfortable. Take down enough tin-pot dictators, and opportunities present themselves. I'm sure that hasn't changed. The spoils of war, my boy. The spoils of war."

Ferguson looked about and behind them, trying to look casual even though every muscle in his body had tightened.

When he saw that no one had been close enough to hear—and not even he was paranoid enough to believe their enemies bugged old age homes—he turned back to Saviano, and leaned as close as he could.

"Are you nuts?" Ferguson said. "Someone could have heard you."

Saviano swatted a dismissive hand through the air. "Relax. This is a place for retired CEOs and CFOs. Former doctors, dentists, and lawyers. They're harmless. Although I must say, one of the CEOs is a real bastard!" He chuckled at his own joke. "Not an enemy agent in the bunch. Enemy agents don't live this long." Saviano boomed with even more laughter, and slapped a hand on his knee.

If not for his training, Ferguson would have shifted uneasily in his seat, his hands grown clammy, and his mouth gone dry. Instead, he looked at Saviano impassively as if nothing at all had happened.

"Sal, you need to—"

The pretty *maître d* who had taken Saviano's name approached, smiling pleasantly. "Mr. Saviano, your table is ready."

Carrying his Cabernet for him, she led them to the dining area and a square table at the far end near the windows, where outside darkness had already fallen. The table was set for four with a white tablecloth and two lighted red candles. Before wheeling away Saviano's walker, she gave them their menus and said, "Your two guests are joining you now."

Ferguson frowned. "I thought it would just be the two of us."

"Nonsense," Saviano said with a dismissive flick of the

wrist, sitting down to Ferguson's right. "They do this to improve social interaction and everyone here is delightful."

Their two guests were both women, both using walkers which the *maître d* also wheeled away. The younger looking of the two was a redhead named Lydia, who had moved in two years earlier. She sat opposite Saviano. The other woman, sitting opposite Ferguson, was a white-haired, excessively thin, frail-looking woman named Theresa. She'd been there five years, but didn't look to Ferguson as though she'd last much longer.

Their waitress, a high school girl named Julie with brown hair tied back in a ponytail, took their drink orders and in almost no time at all returned with the drinks and fresh, warm bread that smelled of oats, and asked if they were ready to order. They were. Along with the associated salads and soups, Lydia ordered the shrimp scampi over angel hair pasta, Theresa the baked stuffed haddock, Saviano the salmon Florentine, and Ferguson the filet mignon, medium rare.

Almost instantly the waitress arrived with Waldorf salads for all but Theresa, who had opted for the Caesar salad, along with bowls of New England clam chowder for all of them but Theresa.

Ferguson dug into the chowder, thick, and rich, and creamy. It tasted delicious, almost as good as Legal's.

Amidst bites of their salads. the two women shared their favorite activities. Though she'd only been there a short time, Lydia had joined the Bridge Club, the Backgammon Club, and the Classical Music Lovers Society. Theresa had cut back to just the Quilting Club and played lots of mahjong. When it got to Saviano's turn, he leaned close and grinned conspiratorially.

"You fine young ladies, I'm going to tell you a wonderful secret," he announced. "Ferguson here is a...*spy!*"

Ferguson choked and half a mouthful of hot clam chowder backed up into his nose.

"Really?" Lydia exclaimed. "How exciting!"

"Like James Bond," Theresa said, sitting across from Ferguson. "Only not as handsome." She blinked and apparently realizing what she'd just said, put the tips of her fingers over her mouth and turned red. "I am *so* sorry!"

"That's quite all right," Ferguson said with a shrug. "Not even my mother would say I'm as handsome as James Bond." And as Theresa tittered, her hand still over her mouth, he added in a conspiratorial whisper, "But I'm not really a spy."

Ferguson tried to get Saviano's eye, but the old man was having none of it.

"The two of us got shot one time during a top secret operation together in Honduras," Saviano said.

The words sent an icy chill up and down Ferguson's spine. They were all too close to the truth. It had been El Salvador, and they'd both gotten shot, he in the shoulder and Saviano in the rear end.

Ferguson grabbed Saviano's thick forearm and squeezed, but not before the old man added, "I took it in the right buttocks."

"Oh my," Lydia and Theresa said in unison.

Ferguson squeezed harder, as if that could choke off the words, but Saviano's forearms were like chiseled granite.

The old man kept grinning and winked. "If you play your cards right, ladies, I just might show it to you."

Lydia blushed and giggled.

"Show what?" Theresa asked.

"His ass!" Lydia answered in a stage whisper, which got them both blushing and giggling like teenagers.

"Could I speak to you privately?" Ferguson said, gritting his teeth and maxing out his pressure on Saviano's arm. He pulled up on the old man's arm, as if to drag him away from the table before realizing Saviano's walker was gone. Not that he, Ferguson, could drag Saviano anywhere he didn't want to go in the first place.

Ferguson released his grip, and settled back in his chair. If he couldn't drag the old man away from the table or muzzle him somehow, what could he do? He'd have to try something else. There was only so much of this talk that could be laughed off and dismissed. Any more, and he'd have to take drastic measures right here, in full view of everyone, and deal with the consequences later.

The solution came to Ferguson when Lydia asked him, "And where did you get hit?"

Ferguson smiled warmly. "I didn't really get hit by a bullet. And I'm not really a spy. It's a fun fantasy, but I'm actually quite boring. I sell life insurance."

"Really? Theresa said, and took a bite of her salad. "How fascinating."

Before Ferguson could marvel at how anyone could consider life insurance fascinating, Saviano jumped in.

"He got hit in the right shoulder. A couple inches the other way..." Saviano shook his head at the wonder of it. "... and Ferguson here would have been a dead man."

"Oh my," the two ladies said again in unison.

"Where did you say this happened?" Lydia asked.

"Brazil," Saviano said emphatically before Ferguson could stop him.

Ferguson stared at Saviano, who didn't seem to notice any more than the two ladies that he'd switched from one erroneous country to another.

Julie, their waitress, approached with a wide, silver, circular tray loaded down with their entrees. She set it down on a stand ten feet behind Saviano, and brought the first plate over.

"Who had the salmon Florentine?" she asked.

Ferguson waited for Saviano to claim his dish, but the old man sat there unmoving, eyes darting about as did the two women, their faces masks of fear, the fear of a student who has shown up for an exam without having studied.

"I'm sorry," Julie said. "I left my order book back in the kitchen. Let me go get it."

Ferguson gestured toward Saviano. "Sal had the salmon."

"Yes! The salmon!" Saviano said in a near gasp of gratitude. "That's right. I had the salmon."

Ferguson added, "Lydia had the shrimp scampi, Theresa ordered the haddock, and I had the filet."

"Yes!" the women exclaimed. Lydia added, "That's right. I'm sure of it. This young man has saved the day."

Ferguson wasn't so sure that sixty-one ranked as young but he supposed that in this audience it did.

"So many of us are having memory issues," Lydia said. "It's a terrible thing. Oh to be young like you."

He began once again to think of a way to cover the

tracks Saviano's motor mouth had left behind when the old man solved the problem.

"Did you know, ladies, that Ferguson here is...a spy?" Saviano asked.

Lydia and Theresa nodded and busied themselves with their food. They had the look of women who had watched this mental deterioration happen to so many others, knowing that someday, the bell of dementia, and maybe even Alzheimer's, might toll for them. So they would not disrespect this man here and point out his failing since they knew it could just as easily be them. Instead, they would act as though they were hearing all this for the first time, even if feigning that same level of surprise was beyond them, because they knew that for Saviano, as far as he knew, he was telling it for the first time.

"We both got shot once," Saviano said, "in Guatemala."

Ferguson wondered if they stayed here long enough, would Saviano complete an entire tour of Latin America, specifying a different country each time, going through all of them except the real one, El Salvador? Probably not. That would be twenty countries.

Well, there wasn't much worry now that these ladies would believe this far-fetched story of spies and getting shot, breaching security. They would dismiss Saviano's words as those of yet another sad dementia case.

"You want to know where I got shot?" Saviano asked. "In the *ass!*" He winked. "And if you play your cards right, ladies, I just might show it to you."

Lydia and Theresa smiled awkwardly, then busily cut their food, as if it had become the most interesting thing in the world.

By the time all of them polished off their entrees and desserts of baked apple pie a la mode, Saviano had repeatedly told of his spying escapades with Ferguson, navigating from the Honduras and Brazil the first time, Guatemala the second, followed by Panama, Bolivia, and Peru.

Ferguson didn't have a worry in the world that either of the ladies believed it.

WHEN THE TWO men got back up to Saviano's apartment on the seventh floor, the old man opened a bottle of Cabernet, and they sat at his small kitchen table, a new one by the looks of it, and using Tiffany crystal wine goblets, toasted to old times and good friends.

"So how is that old bastard, Gallagher?" Saviano asked.

"Still an old bastard," Ferguson said.

He felt badly about what he was going to have to do, but knew it had to be done.

"I would have thought they'd put him out to pasture by now," Saviano said.

"It's a wonder they're keeping any of us old-timers around," Ferguson said. "The new generation is all about technology. Not about brain power and outsmarting the bad guys. It all comes down to an electronic chip that can do this, and another electronic chip that can do that. Not like the old days."

Ferguson wanted to keep talking, to make the end for Saviano as pleasant and as easy as possible. He had to go. There was no question about it at all. Blabbing about one old mission after another left them no choice.

He had to go.

And so Ferguson had palmed the capsule and slipped it into the old man's wine when he wasn't looking. It would be doing the trick any time now. Easy and painless.

Ferguson had thought this was nothing but a shit mission, checking on Saviano like all the guys who had checked on him before, making sure he could still be trusted. It'd be a rubber stamp, he'd thought. Just another shit mission that any flunky could do. Have dinner with the old man. Make sure he still had his marbles.

Well, the old man's body was still good, that barrel chest and Popeye forearms and good looks, but Saviano's mind was going, going, gone.

So the shit mission had turned into an I-gotta-do-a-shitty-thing mission.

Part of the job.

No choice.

But this was a shitty thing.

Just another minute or two. Ferguson sipped his wine.

"I noticed you left out the real country where we got shot," Ferguson said, to pass the time.

"El Salvador," Saviano said, nodding.

"I thought...I thought it was just a subconscious thing what with you..." Ferguson shrugged.

"Me telling the same story five times?" Saviano asked, raising a knowing eyebrow.

"You knew?"

Ferguson tried to get to his feet, but his arms and legs didn't want to work.

"And me forgetting that I ordered salmon Florentine?" Saviano said, shaking his head. "The ladies, Lydia and

Theresa, do have memory issues and they're getting worse, especially Theresa. Not bad enough to think my spy story was new each time, but they're starting to have a tough time. I'm sure it'll happen to me sooner or later, too. But not yet."

Ferguson felt an intense need to urinate. A warmth filled his gut and abdomen. He wondered if he'd already let loose.

"What's going on?" he asked, noting his words were slurred.

"You're not the first one who has come to check on me," Saviano said. "You won't be the last."

"But—"

"You thought you were testing me to see if I was still safe, but the test was a double-edged sword. You were being tested, too."

Ferguson felt the warmth inside his chest about to explode. "But it was supposed to be *you*. You, if you were... if you were a threat."

"I keep going as long as I can outsmart the likes of you," Saviano said. "When I retired, that was my deal with Gallagher, that sonuvabitch. It was really a stroke a genius, if I don't say so myself. He could send me the likes of you, the end-of-the-line cases he thought should be terminated, and if they got the best of me—without employing brutish techniques, of course, since no one is a match for a bullet, a knife, or a garrote—then that would let him know they weren't quite at the end of the line.

"So for Gallagher, this is a win-win. I either thin his herd for him, rid him of all of you over-the-hill types who don't have your fastball anymore, or if you finish me off, then I was a danger he's gotten rid of, and he's gotten proof you still have what it takes. You walk away, knowing it'll look like I've died of natural causes. He calls off the disposal team that's scheduled to arrive with a replacement for my perpetually faulty refrigerator, or with a new piece of furniture, or perhaps—" Saviano licked his lips "—four or five cases of my favorite Cabernet. The team wheels in *something* in a large boxed crate, and leaves with a significantly heavier boxed crate. In your case, about two hundred pounds heavier."

Ferguson wanted to argue that he still had his fastball. That he wasn't ready to get stuffed into a refrigerator or whatever boxed crate was waiting for him.

But his mouth wouldn't work. His mind wasn't doing so well either. It felt like a cloudy, spinning mess.

"Think of it, my friend," Saviano said in a soft, hypnotic voice. "How long has it been since Gallagher gave you a really prime assignment? How long since he trusted you with anything good?"

Forever! Ferguson wanted to shout the word, wanted to scream it. His lips tried to form the letter F but could not.

"Turns out, he was right," Saviano said. "You got sloppy tonight, very sloppy, thinking I was just an old fool." He smiled wanly. "I am not an old fool."

No, he wasn't, Ferguson had to admit, his heart sinking even as the fire in his chest raged and the numbness spread down his legs. *I'm the old fool. He conned me good, and he didn't even have to work at it.*

I haven't just lost my fastball, I've lost my curve and changeup, too.

"But I also am not a cruel man. Better that I send you

off into the night than one of our enemies," Saviano said gently.

Ferguson's eyes felt impossibly heavy. All about the room everything was growing dark and cold.

"And so my friend," Saviano said, "on behalf of our government and that bastard Gallagher, I thank you for your service. Good night, and farewell."

And in the instant before his lights went out for the final time, Ferguson nodded.

MAKONDE TREE OF LIFE

INTRODUCTION TO "MAKONDE TREE OF LIFE"

I usually don't repeat stories from one collection to another. My preference is for readers to be experiencing each story for the first time. (That is, unless they have the good taste to subscribe to the publications in which I frequently appear. To all of you with such wonderfully refined tastes: thank you! I hope you enjoy my stories a second time around!)

With themed collections such as this one, however, that poses a dilemma. Should I leave out a story that perfectly fits the theme, potentially one of my best stories, simply to avoid that repetition? If I do, doesn't that diminish the collection? At the same time, don't I want to avoid repetition to provide my readers with the most bang for their buck?

Yes and yes.

Here's what I've done. I'm in the process of releasing six new collections in the next seven months. (Hey, I gotta fit my suspense novel *Pain Train* in there somewhere. And yeah, I write a lot of short stories. I could fill several additional new collections if I weren't being so damned picky. So please keep an eye out for the five collections that follow this one.)

There will be zero overlap in those six new books. No duplications at all. Where a story could fit in multiple places, this volume won out as the most tightly themed of them all. I can't, however, change the past. I can't remove a story from one of the four collections I published in previous years.

And yet I'm insisting that you receive in these pages the best aging stories I've ever written. What wins, then, the rock or the hard place?

Both, I hope.

I've included this story and two others from previous years' collections because I feel the theme of aging demands their inclusion. What about that bang for the buck baloney? Not baloney at all. You can consider the three "repeats" to instead be "freebies," since the other seven stories by themselves would match the size of my typical collection, both in story count and word count.

The best of both worlds, I think.

I hope you agree. I offer for your consideration, Exhibit A, "*Makonde* Tree of Life."

MAKONDE TREE OF LIFE

*E*dith had forgotten about the ebony wood carving George bought while they were on the African safari. But she forgot about a lot of things these days.

He'd arranged to have it shipped home from Tanzania—the shipping had cost even more than the five-hundred-dollar cost of the admittedly exquisite piece—but he'd suffered a fatal heart attack within a week of their return, two weeks before the package arrived. So she'd tearfully stuffed the unopened two-by-four-foot package marked FRAGILE! GLASS! (even though there wasn't a sliver of glass in the wooden carving) in the back of the bedroom closet, and when she sold their Colonial and moved into an apartment at Bountiful Sunsets retirement home, the still-unopened package went from the back of one closet to the back of another.

It sat there for year after year, tucked behind all the dress clothes Edith never wore anymore but didn't have the heart to throw out. She knew she ought to donate them all to Goodwill or the Salvation Army; the whole lot of them smelled faintly of mothballs. But they were memories of better days, days full of bustling activity, things to do, places to go, and people to meet. Always a need to look at her best, standing next to George with a smile on her face.

Now, she had this nice apartment with a full kitchen, a front room with a TV and a DVR that someone had actually programmed for her, and a carpeted bedroom with a desk, dresser, and a spacious closet.

But to what end?

It didn't matter whether she was dressed to the nines or just wearing her plain white cotton pajamas, as plain as plain can be, as she sat there watching *Wheel of Fortune* and *Jeopardy.*

Who cared? Nobody.

There had been a time when she'd dressed up for Pat Sajak and Vanna as she watched *Wheel of Fortune,* welcoming them into her home (even though, of course, she knew they couldn't see her), and she changed into a different, even classier outfit for Alex Trebek and *Jeopardy,* which aired in the following half hour. She'd eagerly blurt out her answers; she was good.

Not anymore. Now she just watched in her plain white PJs, even putting her feet up on the coffee table. She hardly got any *Jeopardy* questions right or filled in the blanks correctly on *Wheel of Fortune* to spell out the answer. She'd even begun to record *Jeopardy* and re-watch it the next day, sometimes two, three, and four times.

But she *still* couldn't get the answers right. How could she be watching a fourth time in twenty-four hours—*and really paying attention*—and not know the answers?

It was awful.

So it was no surprise that she'd forgotten about George's package, hidden in the back of the closet. But when she saw it—after tripping on the carpet outside the closet, falling down and almost smacking her head on it—it seemed high time to open the damned thing up.

When she pulled the carving out of the package and set it in the middle of her desk, it almost took her breath away. And not just because it reminded her of how much George had loved the piece. Circular and about two feet tall and eight inches wide, the *Makonde* Tree of Life included seven levels of three-inch high figures, two men and two women at each level, their arms interwoven as if they were dancing, each level of four intricately carved figures standing on top of the one below, symbolizing each generation resting atop its predecessors.

It was beautiful. No wonder George had loved it. He so would have enjoyed it in their home had it arrived before his demise.

Edith ran her hand softly along the middle level, stroking the carved, ebony face of the nearest male figure as if it were George himself.

And with only a split second warning, her body was sucked out of the room.

EDITH SENSED THE WATER, fetid and swamp-like, though moving lazily past, an instant before she went under. Down she went, with almost no air in her lungs. She opened her eyes, blinking, disbelieving. Was about to open her mouth for a panicked gulp of air even as she knew she was now two or three feet below. Four or five. Six. Saw only a greenish-brown, silty cloud and large, cow-sized, four-legged creatures thrashing about in the same state of panic she felt.

She touched the squishy bottom, for a second felt herself getting sucked down into it, half of her ankle submerged and embedded and then all of it, the muck inching up her leg, prompting an instinctive scream she only held back by the barest of margins.

But then she touched a hard bottom. Wiggling loose of the muck, staring wild-eyed through the green-brown, pea-soup-thick silt, trying to make sense of what had become of her, Edith pushed off the bottom and shot to the surface.

She broke through an instant before her lungs could hold out no longer and took an agonized gasp of air. She bobbed for a second at the surface, her legs kicking furiously, and then the stench hit her like a hard, wet slap across the face. The coppery smell of blood and death and rotting carcasses filled her nostrils. An instant later, one of the four-legged beasts—a wide-eyed wildebeest, its flank the distinctive stripes of brown and black, all of six hundred pounds while rising five feet high, not even counting the neck and head—rose somehow out of the water and toppled over, slamming against Edith, driving her down with it back below the surface.

Edith flailed even as the wildebeest kicked its mighty legs, once striking her in the right thigh, sending a shooting pain up and down the leg. Only then did she see the massive crocodile, easily fifteen feet long if not twenty, a giant weighing in at perhaps two tons. This was what had propelled the wildebeest up out of the water before dragging it back down now, its jaws clamped tight about the wildebeest's snout.

Wildly, Edith pushed away from the thrashing beast. She stared at its panicked eyes, eyes that told of the wildebeest's instinctive knowledge of its impending death. And though her own fear was almost every bit as palpable, she instinctively reached out to the dying creature, as if any gesture of sympathy or comfort she could offer would help it even as the crocodile dragged it down to drown it.

Edith's head broke above the water's surface a second time. Below her, the two giant creatures thrashed, the water a bubbling maelstrom of death. In front of her, less than twenty feet away, more wildebeests and a few braying zebras stampeded across the river, the column of them seven or eight wide, forced ahead by more of their kind behind them pushing them onward even into their deaths, the parade stretching to the far bank and its sandy slope upward to the plains eight or ten feet above. From the opposite bank, more crocodiles left their sunny, sandy banks, sliding into the waters for their next meal.

And as Edith swam away from them toward the far shore with young, strong arms, she realized with amazement that she was viewing the Great Migration, one of the great wonders of the world in which almost two million wildebeests, zebras, and other creatures migrated from the southern Serengeti up to this northern part—this must be the Mare River—where the creatures would cross from Tanzania into Kenya.

She and George had been too early for the Great Migration. Impossible to time precisely, they'd missed it by three weeks, a great disappointment to both of them.

Well, she was seeing it now, far more up close and personal than she had ever wished.

Behind her, a single cloven hoof broke through the water, and then another and another, until eventually all four of them poked through, followed by the rest of the legs, the ill-fated wildebeest now dead and drowned, lying on its back, its stiff legs pointed to the heavens.

Edith thought of the panicked look in its eyes and stroked harder for the shore.

EDITH STARED at the ebony carving resting on the bedroom desk. Her heart hammered. Her hands shook. She stood there, her plain, white pajamas dripping wet, water pooling on the carpet beneath her.

What had just happened? Or more accurately, had what she thought had just happened really happened?

Of course not.

She didn't believe in any of that crazy stuff on the TV nowadays. UFOs. Time travel. Telekinesis. She might be losing her marbles—okay, she most assuredly was losing her marbles—but she wasn't so far gone that she believed that by stroking this ebony piece of African art, magnificent as it might be, she had somehow been transported to the northernmost edge of Tanzania.

Into the Mara River just as the Great Migration had taken almost two million wildebeest and a couple hundred thousand zebras to the edge of the river for the crossing to the other side.

Into the middle of an attack on a hapless wildebeest by

the most gigantic crocodile she had ever seen—its immense bulk even larger than the most massive one she and George had seen on safari years ago from the safety of their SUV.

It was impossible.

And yet, she tugged at her sopping wet pajamas, pulling them away from her wet skin. How had she gotten wet, if not from the Mara River?

But, of course, she could have stepped into the shower with her PJs on, couldn't she? It wouldn't exactly be the most crazy thing she'd done lately. It was certainly easier to believe that in some inexplicable fugue she'd stepped in, turned on the water, and imagined the most exciting of adventures.

An amazing adventure to spice up her hopelessly mundane, pathetically boring existence.

Of course. It made all the sense in the world. It would also explain why her hair was tangled and wet. And it would certainly make sense that the horrible taste in her mouth wasn't from the foul silt in the Mara River, but rather that it was all in her a-few-marbles-short-of-a-full-load brain.

It didn't matter that she'd never possessed so much as a mosquito's imagination. This wasn't imagination or creativity.

It was full-blown dementia. She was halfway down Alzheimer's Avenue.

She couldn't, of course, tell anyone. They'd send her to Fully Assisted Living and the name of Edith Rathbone would join those avoided here in polite conversion, after spoken once with sad, downcast eyes.

It was only when she stripped out of her pajamas to step

into the shower, presumably for the *second* time, that she saw it.

Her heart skipped a beat, and her hands became clammy.

There on her right thigh was a bruise forming of an unmistakable shape.

The imprint of a wildebeest's cloven hoof.

DESPITE HER USUAL SLEEPING PILLS, Edith spent the night tossing and turning, sure the immense bulk of the crocodile was lying in bed, beneath the sheets, beside her. It would drag her down to the foul depths of the Mara River to drown her, leaving her to float on the surface, hands and legs extended to the African sky. She couldn't quiet the urgent grunts she still heard of the horned wildebeest or rid her mind of the look of panicked fear in its eyes.

Shouldn't her own eyes show the same fear, her fate every bit as much doomed?

Time after time, she ran her hand over her right thigh, feeling beneath her thin, plain white cotton pajamas—she owned multiple pairs—the outline of the cloven-shaped bruise.

When she finally crawled out of bed, she didn't even think about breakfast. She peed, took her five medications only out of the most instinctive reflex, then bolted back to her desk where the *Makonde* Tree of Life rested in its center. She gazed in wonder at the figures, the three-inch-high ebony men and women.

Had this really transported her to her African adventure

last night, causing her to miss Pat and Vanna and Alex? Could it do so again?

Edith reached out a hand to stroke it in the way a lover strokes the soft side of the face of the one they find most dear. The way she had stroked George's face and he had so often stroked hers.

She ran her fingertips along the indentations in the smooth, ebony wood, stroking once again the closest male figure's cheeks in the middle level.

For a moment, Edith thought she was about to faint, her sense of lightheadedness making her weave unsteadily in her chair. But then—

She was gone.

EDITH SAT ON THE GROUND, still clad in her plain white, cotton pajamas, surrounded by a sea of thick, dry, brown, foot-high grass. It was warm, but not inordinately so, and she remembered how it had been that way throughout their safari due to the Serengeti's elevation. Slowly, in amazement, she got to her feet. The skin on her ankles and bare feet felt scratchy in the dry grass, but she ignored it.

This had to be the Ngorogoro Crater, a hundred square miles of the most abundant life on the planet, once a volcano that rose perhaps as high as Kilimanjaro but exploded and collapsed in on itself and was now a crater two thousand feet deep. In the distance, she could see its rim, rising in the mist. Close by, less than a hundred feet away, Thomson gazelles sprang to and fro, thirty or forty in all, elegant with their crooked horns and ornate black-and-yellow striping. Suddenly, the whole flock of them, stopped, looked off to Edith's left and bolted.

Edith squinted, but could see nothing in the bright noontime sunlight. She wondered if maybe, just maybe, this would be her chance to make up for the safari's one disappointment. She and George had seen all the big game and all the great sites but one: the great rhinoceros. It had been hunted into near extinction by poachers for its horns, thought by some to have mystical powers ranging from sexual performance to curing cancer. Even inside the national parks. Their tour guides had tried valiantly, but there was no manufacturing an appearance.

Maybe...

As if her wish had conjured an appearance, one began to trot slowly into sight from off to her left. Edith thought about bolting like the gazelles. Her body felt young and energized, full of life, nothing like the bag of flab and bones she'd left back in her apartment. And she certainly knew that safari-goers caught out of their vehicles often met a painful death, an easy meal for the many predators here, but where could she run to?

There was no safe vehicle to sprint for. There was no hole to climb in. Surely any holes were occupied by some form of life that would not welcome her appearance.

Besides, she'd been an arm's length away from a two-ton crocodile attacking a horned wildebeest that outweighed her by about three times and had come away with only the cloven-hoofed bruise. At no point had the crocodile or perhaps the wildebeest even known she existed. The same held true for the Thomson gazelles happily oblivious to her presence, spooked only by the approaching rhino. What might be safest was to pretend she was invisible, and not move a muscle.

So Edith just stood and watched in her plain white pajamas and bare feet as the gray, horned beast with thick, armored skin approached, no longer trotting, just moving slowly toward her, in no hurry at all, stopping to pluck some greenery out of the brown grassland and chew on it.

Until finally it stood a mere ten feet away.

It was *huge*. Edith had always associated elephants with massive size, and they were larger than rhinos, but good God, this beast was *immense*. Its shoulders towered over her, easily over six feet high. It had to be almost fifteen feet long, and probably weighed close to two tons. It smelled a lot like circuses she'd gone to as a child, and that did make her wrinkle her nose just a bit, but really, who cared? This creature was magnificent! Its leathery skin looked impenetrable—what could kill this thing, other than, of course, humans?—but what she couldn't take her eyes off was that massive front horn. It had two of them, but the larger front one had to be four feet long. Even the shorter back horn had to be a foot-and-a-half long.

A four-foot long horn!

She'd always been short, only a few inches over five feet tall (and losing fractions of those inches every year), but this beast's horn was more than three-quarters her height.

Edith clenched her eyes closed, sure she was imagining all of this, sure that somewhere up above George was laughing at her obsession with the size of the horn, equating it to her undeniable sexual frustration.

But when she opened her eyes, she was still here,

standing in the grasslands of the Ngorogoro Crater, staring at the rhino's four-foot long horn.

She wanted to creep closer and touch it, but somehow felt that would be wrong. This whole blessing, courtesy of the *Makonde* Tree of Life—unless, of course, it was just courtesy of her dropping one last vital marble in a brain that could no longer even cheat at *Jeopardy*—seemed to dictate that only the wildlife here could initiate contact, not her.

The leathery rhino stepped closer. And then closer still, until she could reach out and touch it.

But she didn't.

Instead, it nibbled at a piece of greenery between her toes, its lips grazing her big right toe as it did, tickling it. All the while, the massive horn swung back and forth. Crazily, Edith thought of her long-since passed mother saying, "That thing will poke your eye out!" And Edith, half afraid it would, leaned back to avoid the huge thing.

Instead, the horn caught on the bottom cuff of her left pajama leg, and as the rhino lifted its head, tore the pant leg all the way up to her knee.

Edith yelped. She couldn't help it. She'd sworn she wouldn't move, not even with the rhino's lips tickling her toes, and she wouldn't utter a sound, but she couldn't help it.

For a moment, she thought the rhino was looking at her, and maybe it even blinked. Was it making some sort of contact? Sending some sort of message?

Apparently not, because it just turned and ambled off, its huge bulk swaying as it did. When the distance separating them reached fifty feet, Edith slowly began to follow, but then it broke into a trot, and she could not keep pace.

And as soon as it was gone from sight, Edith felt something pulling her away from the Ngorogoro Crater with a loud sucking sound. She instinctively fell to the ground and grasped hold of the thick, dry grass, clinging to it desperately, not wanting to leave, not wanting ever to leave, but the grass roots pulled free and she found herself zooming quickly away.

Back to her apartment at Bountiful Sunsets, where her left pajama leg was most definitely torn up the side all the way to her knee.

ON HER NEXT TRIP, Edith raced for a split second alongside a cheetah, her legs young and strong, but no match for the world's fastest mammal. The time after that, she began dressing up for her trips—no more plain white PJs for her or for Africa. And with her wearing a bright yellow flowered blouse and tan slacks, elephants stampeded past her, the ground shaking beneath her feet as they passed. And the time after that, three lionesses took down a Thomson gazelle no more than five feet away from her, then moved aside and let the male lion feast first, crunching loudly on the gazelle bones.

And so it went, always something new, always something wonderful, whether it was arriving at night and hunting with the hyenas, their orange eyes glowing in the pitch black darkness, shrieking their bone-chilling laughter, or swimming in the filthy waters with three-thousand-pound hippos, the stench almost overwhelming, but the experience filled with excitement, filled with *life*.

It never grew old.

Unlike life back at Bountiful Sunsets, which was all about growing old. That life held no more interest for Edith. Not even Pat and Vanna and Alex.

And certainly not going down to the dining hall to eat dinner with all the other nearly-dead members of Bountiful Sunsets. Edith took to having her dinner sent to her room instead of going down to the dining hall, as was her right, so the only time she left her apartment was to visit the savannahs of the Serengeti.

It was, after all, the only thing *worth* leaving her apartment for.

And after a time, she couldn't be bothered to prepare the other two meals each day, as was expected of those on the one-meal-a-day plan. And sometimes, she even forgot to eat the dinner brought to her apartment each night.

A bothersome doctor, a young little snot of a woman with short hair, big glasses, and a big attitude even though she was barely out of medical school and was about as interesting to listen to as cardboard, asked about Edith's diet, since she was losing a lot of weight. The doctor wanted to run tests, but Edith refused. She was ridding herself of the Bountiful Bulge, the phrase used by residents to talk about their increased weight since arriving, and the tests could wait for her next regularly scheduled appointment.

Lions, rhinos, hippos, and elephants didn't need medical intervention and neither did she.

Edith looked at her increasingly gaunt features in the mirror. Well, if fashion models could take skeletal figures to an extreme—they weren't much more than skin and bones, were they?—then why not her?

She undressed and stood naked before the bedroom full-length mirror.

Good, Lord. Did she have any muscle mass left at all? Her wrinkled skin just hung there, about all that was left beside the protruding bones. How far under a hundred pounds was she now?

How far under ninety?

Could she have dipped below eighty?

No, of course not. Well, probably not. She was pretty sure if she stood on that bathroom scale—something she had no intention of doing at all, right at that instant—the first digit would be at least an eight.

She'd have to start eating better soon. She'd even put it on her calendar for tomorrow. It would be a priority.

But that was tomorrow.

Today still beckoned, and Edith looked forward to spending it under African skies. Still naked, not even realizing it, she tottered over to the *Makonde* Tree of Life. A smile stretched across her weathered face as she reached out to caress it

THE THICK, WET CLOUD OF MEMORY

INTRODUCTION TO "THE THICK, WET CLOUD OF MEMORY"

My wife's grandparents lived long lives. Her grandmother remained sharp as a tack into her mid-nineties, joyful and spry, always offering cookies or other snacks, always ready for another game of Skip-Bo. She'd laugh uproariously when she won, which was often, and then beg for another game, no matter how late it had become. She drew on a seemingly boundless supply of energy and mental acuity. She suffered no decline at all until the final few weeks of her life.

We should all be so lucky.

My wife's grandfather, on the other hand, a sweet man in his own right, struggled with dementia in his final years. He'd fail to recognize his own son and in fact, feared that this total stranger had come to steal his wife away from him.

A fear of such a future gets me fretting every time I forget someone's name or make even the most minor mental misstep. I can practically hear the marbles I'm losing clanking on the floor, the sound deafening and ominous.

I haven't lost them all. There are admittedly a few of

them still bouncing around inside my noggin—yeah, I can hear them rattle every time I turn my head, ha ha ha, not funny—and I know I'm overreacting to an utterly *absurd* degree. After all, I still teach advanced computer science courses two or three nights a week after spending most days having a wonderful time making stuff up for you readers.

I'm still using that noggin pretty much from the time I climb out of bed to the time I slide back in. In fact, my sweet wife, Brenda, sometimes wishes I'd shut that noggin off for a bit. Give my poor brain a break. (And I suppose, give her a break, too.)

Even so, Willard's plight in this story still makes it a horror story for me from the very first words. And, I think, for us all.

THE THICK, WET CLOUD OF
MEMORY

Willard sits at the head table, his crimson bowtie tight against his neck, his white shirt uncomfortably tight, and his black suit jacket snug in the shoulders. Beside him, Edna looks like Zsa Zsa Gabor, dressed to the nines in her nicest dark blue party dress, long dangling earrings, sparkling necklace, and her hair made up fancy thanks to three hours at the beauty salon. Even as the lingering smells of baked chicken, tomato sauce, and red wine fill the air, a three-layer cake with white icing and a basketball-sized gold decoration with "90" in the middle is wheeled out in front of him on the other side of the fifty-foot long head table.

The Knights of Columbus hall is filled with rows of circular tables, six people to each, radiating out from an open, wooden dance floor. The hall buzzes with loud conversation and peals of laughter. Edna tells him these are all friends and relatives, almost two hundred in all, some of whom flew cross country just for the celebration.

But they all look like strangers to Willard. He can't find a face he recognizes.

Is this a surprise party? He grimly supposes it has to be. At this stage of his life, everything's a surprise.

"We're going to have a receiving line now so all of you can come up and congratulate Willard on his ninetieth birthday," a DJ booms from loudspeakers to both sides. He stands on a small platform to the left, not more than thirty years old, pudgy with a glittering earring and even a disgusting nose ring. "So if his lovely wife Edna can join him there beside the cake, we'll get this started.

"We won't expect that Willard will be able to remain standing for all of you, so don't be disappointed if he's seated by the time you get there. There are, after all, almost two hundred of you here wishing him well on this wonderful day. Give yourselves a round of applause!"

Willard gets to his feet and leaning heavily on his cane and with Edna on his other arm, hobbles around the end of the head table into position in front of the large cake.

Be careful, he reminds himself, mindful that while that last glass of wine he drank eased his anxiety over this event, there's a distinct possibility the wine eased it too much. The cloud in his mind hangs especially thick and wet—he knows *none* of these people!—and he still clings to a sense of dread that he will make a fool of himself, giving everyone a lasting memory of him that will tarnish, if not wipe out entirely, all the dignified and honorable memories from his ninety long years.

He's even worn a diaper—the indignity of it!—even though incontinence is close to the last of his problems, because, as he's tried to warn himself so many times, you can never be too careful.

But it all goes well until almost the very end. Edna whispers each person's name and how he's supposed to know them as they approach. *Our daughter Susan and her third husband, Lewis.*

That's enough for Willard. He doesn't ask what happened to the first two husbands. It doesn't matter whether they both divorced her or she threw them out of skyscraper windows. He doesn't need to know. He's being careful, the red wine notwithstanding.

Daughter Susan, check. Husband Lewis, check.

Willard will get through this with his dignity intact. He's sure of it. He'll even manage without sitting down once in the chair that's waiting ten feet behind him, if needed. He's leaning more and more heavily on his cane, leaning with his left arm instead of the usual right so he can shake hands, but even though Edna suggests he sit down, he shakes his head no emphatically. This is likely the last time most of these friends and relatives—*"strangers!"* he hisses before silencing the thought—it's the last they'll see of him, so he swears he will make it a good memory.

A dignified memory of him standing proud and tall to greet every last one of them.

And no one but Edna and those who have visited in recent months—*years?* he wonders—will know about the thick, wet cloud in his mind, will know that he's faking recognition of almost every last one of them.

Strangers.

He's going to make it.

And he does. Until Edna whispers, "Your great-grandson Jeffrey and his fiancée, Lisa."

Willard shakes Jeffrey's hand, smiles, and says what he's said to every single person who's preceded this red-headed, freckled great-grandson. "Thank you so much for coming. It means so much to me."

And then he sees the fiancée, Lisa.

Willard's eyes widen and he almost faints.

"It can't be!" he gasps.

She's a beautiful girl. Early twenties, twenty-four at the oldest. Long, flowing black hair that reaches several inches below her shoulders. A trim figure, accentuated by a clinging, short black dress. Earrings with a small diamond at their center and a matching necklace.

But none of that is what is sending Willard's heart into palpitations and his blood pressure soaring.

It is her face. Long and angular with a model's high cheekbones and thin nose. Eyes of brightest green. And a beautiful smile with bright white teeth straight out of a toothpaste advertisement.

It is from her face that he recognizes her. Her face burns a searing hole through the thick, wet cloud of his memory. Her face tells him that she must be a ghost come back to haunt him for his vilest sin, to unmask him for all the world to see.

"I didn't mean to hit you," he says to her, his voice quivering, his hands shaking violently. "I'm so very, very sorry."

The boy—was it Jeffrey, his name?—laughs and gives Willard a comforting pat on the arm. "You didn't hit her, great-grampy," he says. "You couldn't have. She's never met you before."

Edna touches his arm. "Willard. You should sit down." To someone else, she says, "Get him some water."

But the girl, the ghost, so young, younger than Willard remembers, stares back at him in wide-eyed shock.

"It happened so fast," he says, needing to explain to this phantasm, needing to rid himself of the guilt. "I couldn't react in time. I tried to miss you, but I couldn't."

A voice inside Willard's head tells him to shut his damned mouth, shut it before it's too late. It might already be too late. He must be careful. Not say another word or all might be lost.

But Willard can't stay silent, not with this ghost from his nightmares standing before him.

Accusing him with her look.

He must explain.

"I wasn't drunk," he says, ignoring Edna's hand on his arm, trying unsuccessfully to steer him away. He ignores Edna's words that he doesn't know what he's saying, because he knows *exactly* what he's saying. This is one of the very few things he's been sure about ever since the dark, thick, wet cloud descended on his mind. He knows what he's saying for a certainty. "Not a drop of alcohol. I just didn't see you. It was late. It was dark."

The girl puts a hand up to open mouth, and Willard prepares for a scream.

"I've never driven since," he tries to explain. "My hands were shaking so bad, I barely made it home from the... from the 7-Eleven. On the corner of Chestnut and Tenney, right?"

But he doesn't need to ask. He knows. There are many

things Willard can't remember, almost everything since the cloud descended.

But this one memory, sadly, he can't forget. He *knows* it was the 7-Eleven on the corner of Chestnut and Tenney.

"No!" the girl says, gasping as if she can't breathe, a feeling that seizes Willard, too.

"Yes!" he says, his chest tight but unable to stop. "I couldn't tell anyone. I felt so bad, so guilty, so *awful*. I stopped driving the very next day, I swear it. Ask anyone."

Willard turns and sees Edna staring at him in shock, open-mouthed, disbelieving. Shame covers her face, something he's never seen before, even after his greatest embarrassments.

"What's the date..." the girl begins, her words jagged as she stifles a cry. But then she turns away from him, as if she can't bear to look, and asks Edna, "When did your husband stop driving?"

Edna blinks, surprised at the question, then hesitates. But she answers, her strained face showing hope that perhaps what she says will exonerate her husband of sixty-seven years.

"He had just turned eighty-two, so that would have been about eight years ago." She appears ready to say more, but then stops.

"What month?" the girl asks.

"November," Willard says, and although all the alarm bells in his head are clanging and flashing *be careful, you fool!* in bright blood-red letters, *be careful, you fool!* wildly off and on, he continues. "November 5. I am so, so sorry."

"You killed my mother!" the girl screams at a decibel level that threatens to shatter his eardrums, but most certainly rips open his heart. "You hit her and left her in the street dying! Eight years ago, on November 5. A day that ruined my entire family's lives."

Willard stares at her. "Your mother?"

Now he can see it. See that this girl is not a ghost, but the pretty daughter of the woman he left in the street, no longer pretty herself that night, covered in her own blood. He'd rushed not to get help, but to the nearest automatic car wash so no one could point the finger at him.

In an otherwise honorable life, it had been his one descent into inexcusable evil. His car escaped without a scratch. The woman died. No one ever knew.

The hole in the thick, wet cloud—burned through by the searing memory of that night—widens, and a beam of bright sunlit clarity shows him that years ago, as the cloud began to descend and thicken, he tried to tell his future self to be careful, to safeguard this deepest, darkest secret and keep it wrapped tightly in his disintegrating mind for no one else to see.

He told himself over and over that he must be careful and say nothing of that night, repeating the words *be careful* until they could not be forgotten no matter how much his mind deteriorated. In that way, he would take that awful memory to the grave with him, never besmirching his honor, never losing the dignity of ninety years well and honorably lived.

Except for that one unforgiveable night.

No one else would know. No one else *could* know.

Except him.

And then the day came when not even *he* remembered. The thick, wet cloud blanketed even that memory.

Until this girl came to him, at first appearing to be a phantasm that ripped the dark memory from its hiding place and thrust it in his face. In the end, no phantasm, only a mortal.

A daughter robbed of her mother.

And together, they took that ugliest, darkest secret and in what was almost certainly his final public moment, held it out on display for all to see.

Unmasked for what he truly is, Willard stares about the room. He sees horrified looks from all these strangers, some of whom, with the thick, wet cloud parted and his dark secret released, he actually begins to recognize.

They stare at him and he stares back. He knows he is infinitely more horrified than they are.

He looks over to Edna and sees on her face, where there had once only been love and devotion, the worst look of all: contempt.

Willard suddenly feels so very tired. Bone tired.

"I've got to sit down," he says.

But before he can, the girl, the daughter of the woman he struck and left abandoned, shrieks, "You killed my mother and left her there, you heartless bastard!"

And she gives him an angry, contempt-filled, two-handed shove.

Willard windmills his arms, his cane flying high up in the air, and staggers backward.

His fragile body hits the hard wooden floor, face up, with an audible snap. A second or two later, the cane follows, clattering hollowly.

Pain shoots through Willard's hip and down into his tingling toes. He doesn't need a doctor or X-rays to tell him what he already knows. He has broken his hip. And at his age, as he has noted so many times, a broken hip is a surefire gateway to the grave.

He's a goner. This useless husk of what he once was is about to blow away.

He looks up from the floor at all the wide-eyed, horrified faces looking down on him. Edna gets down on her knees and asks if he's all right, compassion already leaking into what had fleetingly been her contempt-filled face.

Willard's eyes, however, lock onto the girl, her eyes still filled with righteous, fiery anger.

An avenging angel, Willard thinks.

But if he has indeed stepped into the gateway to the grave, then all things considered, he supposes the girl is an angel of mercy as well.

Undeserved mercy.

And for that, Willard thanks her.

THE AMAZING RBG

INTRODUCTION TO "THE AMAZING RBG"

Is this story dated and irrelevant? I'll argue with all my might that it is not. In fact, as I write here in a tumult-filled 2024, it might be more relevant than ever.

To be sure, it was written while Supreme Court Justice Ruth Bader Ginsburg was still alive and kicking, and so many of her disciples feared precisely what the heroine in this story fears. As it turned out, Justice Ginsburg, the real-life Amazing RBG, passed away before the story could be published. Dean Wesley Smith had bought the story, calling it "the perfect *Pulphouse* story," but the pandemic hit and prompted a pause in the magazine's publishing schedule. By the time it resumed, Justice Ginsburg sadly was no more.

Dean was undeterred. In the magazine's introduction to the story, he lamented that the story couldn't appear earlier but said it was "just as strong, maybe stronger. It is not a story you will soon forget."

I agree. I walked a fiction-writing tightrope with this story. Did I pull it off? Does it still work these years later?

I'll let you decide.

THE AMAZING RBG

The woman formerly known as Mildred Hodges, alone in her two-bedroom apartment at Sunset Village, a retirement home an hour north of Boston, leaned into her walker and tottered out of her bedroom. She wore a threadbare white bathrobe over plain white pajamas. Her white hair, now so thin her scalp was visible, stuck up in every direction. Thick-lensed granny glasses adorned the weary face of a woman soon to turn ninety.

She wrinkled her nose. The place smelled of urine. It *always* smelled of urine these days. She'd have to get that looked into.

She pushed herself through the living room, her slippered feet dragging noisily across the dark blue carpet. She felt no temptation at all to turn on the TV. In the past, before George passed, she'd have it on to catch the news while she made coffee for the two of them. These days, however, the news just made her angry.

Angry and afraid for the country.

It also made her even more determined to hang on, but

she didn't need the news for that. Oh, she was going to hang on, all right.

She was going to outlast the monster in the White House.

No, she didn't need the news to give her extra motivation for that. That came with every breath she took. The anger, however—the incredulous, what-the-hell-is-going-on anger—wasn't good for her blood pressure. So the TV stayed off.

She made herself a strong cup of black coffee, placed it on the seat six inches beneath her walker's handlebars, and made her way into her home office. She angled the walker next to the chair behind the large oak desk, placed her coffee mug on a coaster, and sat down. Sunlight streamed in the window behind her that overlooked a flowered courtyard. The other three walls were lined with shelves, filled end-to-end with books, most of them George's. It had been George's office until the cancer took him two years ago.

He'd been a partner at Freeman, Jenkins, and Hodges, specializing in corporate law, whatever that was. All Mildred knew was that it involved corporations paying her husband a lot of money. George had kept his hand in the business even after supposedly retiring, spending an hour or two a couple days a week in this office, either to make it a tax write-off or just to keep himself preoccupied and busy when Mildred wanted him to go somewhere he didn't want to go.

Mildred had needed no office herself back then. Her career had been as a housewife and an administrative assistant, and no one needed a home office for that.

But she damned well needed an office now. The fate of the country depended on it. She had to outlast the monster.

She'd thought she would follow George straight into the ground, six feet under, right after he died. Had almost asked the funeral director for a two-for-one special, she was so sure of it. She'd been "George's wife" and nothing more for so long that when he passed, there didn't seem much left of her. They'd had no kids. That hadn't been possible after... The Mistake.

So there was nothing much left of her at all.

She had never been a great mind, a great conversationalist, a great beauty, or a great anything. Only a great wife, if she'd even been that. And that was gone as soon as they lowered George into the ground.

She was no more important than a bowl of Cheerios. A whole lot of zeroes. Perhaps they were O's for everyone else, not zeroes, but for Mildred they were unquestionably zeroes.

That's all she was. Perhaps all she'd ever been.

Not much of a reason to keep going.

After the first year alone in the painfully empty, far-too-spacious apartment, Mildred knew she couldn't go on that way. Rarely leaving the apartment, hearing little more than the echo of her own voice. Doing little more than watch TV or just stare blankly into space. She didn't know the day of the week. The month of the year. What she had done five minutes before. Whether she'd taken her meds or had already taken them twice or maybe even a dangerous third time.

She didn't give a rat's ass.

Her doctor suggested a caregiver, really just a glorified

nurse, so she hired Deena. But it didn't make a difference. Sure, there was someone to talk to, to handle any medical emergencies, and to dispense her meds so Mildred didn't overdose or underdose.

But it didn't help.

It was all slipping away for Mildred. She was on a precipice, barely holding onto a cliff face, legs dangling above the dark abyss, bloodied fingertips slipping, slipping, slipping.

She could see no reason to hold on.

Until one day her muddled, deteriorating mind imagined what it would be like to be important. To really *make a difference*. To maybe even be famous, in a good way.

And after floating from one notable character to another, finding them nothing special in the grand scheme of things, she latched onto the person of Rachel Bansfield Griffin, the Supreme Court justice. The oldest and most frail member of the Supreme Court's shrinking liberal wing. An icon.

What must it be like to be Rachel Bansfield Griffin? To defend the rights of women and the downtrodden against the barbarian horde? To matter. To really, truly make a difference.

To have a reason to keep going.

Rachel Bansfield Griffin.

To be adored by those who agree with you. To be reviled by those who don't. To make a difference.

Rachel Bansfield Griffin!

Rachel Bansfield Griffin was even referred to in some circles half-humorously as the Amazing RBG. How wonderful to be referred to as Amazing?

Rachel Bansfield Griffin.

And so, in the diminished, deteriorating mind of Mildred Hodges—whether due to insanity or the onset of dementia or even Alzheimer's—Mildred Hodges *became* Rachel Bansfield Griffin.

She was no longer Mildred Hodges. Never again would be. She was Rachel Bansfield Griffin.

The Amazing RBG.

RACHEL, nee Mildred, was poring over her papers by the time Deena let herself into the apartment and appeared in the doorway to the office. A heavyset woman with a bright, toothy smile and brown hair tied up in a bun, Deena chose office attire more like that of a nurse than a Supreme Court justice's clerk: blue scrubs, day after day. But it was a peculiarity the Amazing RBG was willing to overlook. So long as Deena looked professional in court and any public appearances, the peccadillo hurt no one.

"How are you doing this morning, Mrs. H?" Deena asked.

The Amazing RBG looked up from the papers stacked about the desk and glared. She wasn't in court right now, so there was no need for her clerk to call her "Your honor." This was a working office, after all. It wasn't even necessary to call her Ms. or Mrs. Griffin. Hearing the casual "Mrs. G" from a subordinate would be perfectly fine.

But it was time to nip in the bud this constant use each morning of the initial from her old name. Not acceptable.

"*H?*" she said icily.

Deena pursed her lips. She closed her eyes and bowed her head slightly, either to show deference or to muster courage for her defense. "Mrs. Hodges, I really think—"

"The name is Rachel!" the Amazing RBG snapped. "Or Mrs. Griffin. Or Mrs. G. If you can't manage one of those, then you'll have to call me 'Your Honor,' whether this is a courtroom or not. Do you understand me? Unless, of course, you'd prefer, the Amazing RBG."

Deena said nothing, but her troubled eyes spoke volumes.

"Or I'll find another clerk."

"I'm not a clerk. I'm your—"

"You're certainly not much of a clerk, I'll say that! Do you think Neil Gorsuch's clerk would be insolent enough to call him by anything other than his proper name? Do you think Sam Alito's clerk would try to get away with it? Or Clarence Thomas's clerk?"

Deena's shoulders slumped.

"If you can't at least call me Mrs. G or Rachel, I'll find someone who will. Some bright-eyed, bushytailed candidate at Yale or Harvard who'll be willing to give his left nut, or her left tit, to clerk for a Supreme Court justice. You're one of the luckiest people alive. Do you understand me?"

Deena nodded in resignation. "Yes, Mrs. G."

"Now, what did your research uncover in *Johansson v. District of Columbia*?"

"I..." Deena shook her head. "I'm still working on it."

"Insolent," the Amazing RBG said. "And incompetent, too."

She felt bad for being so harsh and demanding, but didn't this clerk understand the stakes? The forces of good were being outflanked and outnumbered by the forces for evil. Only their greatest and most brilliant efforts would win the day. Mediocrity would doom them all.

"You do have an exercise appointment in the pool, Mrs.... Mrs. G," Deena said. She gestured at the papers on the desk. "I know you're very busy, but... exercise is very important."

"Yes, it is," the Amazing RBG admitted grudgingly. She sipped her coffee. "You're right. It's vital if I'm going to outlast the monster."

"The monster?"

"The one in the White House. Haven't you been paying any attention to anything I say? To anything on the news? That Nazi would like nothing better than for me to keel over dead from a cardiac arrest. Then he can replace me with another one of his right wing nuts, and destroy for decades what little is left of the court's balance. I'm sure he's lusting over that possibility right now."

"I'll take you to the pool," Deena said, "to help you outlast the monster." She took a deep breath and forced a smile. "But you'll need to shower first. Pool rules. And um... you've... I think you've forgotten to change your overnight diaper."

The Amazing RBG blinked. Maybe she had. It would certainly explain that smell of urine. "Then I suppose you'll need to help me. Consider it penance for your insolence."

AFTER THE POOL SESSION, the Amazing RBG felt quite invigorated. The smell of chlorine sure beat that of urine.

She was poring over the law books, looking for precedents in *Johansson v. District of Columbia,* when Deena brought up the possible need to move her to the Memory Unit.

"They'll be able to give you the extra care you need," Deena said. "I'm not sure I'm up to the challenge anymore."

"The Memory Unit!" the Amazing RBG thundered. "*The Memory Unit!*"

What a traitor that Deena was! Even suggesting such a thing! What a backstabbing, insubordinate ingrate. The Memory Unit was where the dementia patients got sent, never to return. Never again to mingle with the rest of the population.

A one-way trip to Hell.

The court would hear opening arguments soon. There was no way she, the Amazing RBG, could still function, or even provide the illusion of functioning, if she'd been exiled to the Memory Unit. The mere mention of that possibility would send the Nazi in the White House into a near orgasm. He'd begin compiling lists of replacements, if those lists weren't already finalized. Hell, he'd probably start calling the candidates.

No, she was the Amazing RBG. She had to hold on.

"You listen to me," she said to Deena, wagging her finger. "I may not be totally myself anymore, but I'm close enough. I'm not going anywhere until that evil man is out of the White House. He's not going to replace me with one of his kind. They'll let corporations take over the country. Hell, if he's able to replace me and maybe one more justice, they'll even overturn *Roe v. Wade.* Next thing you'll know, there'll be a whole lot of girls like me."

The Amazing RBG gasped. She'd said it out loud. Referred to The Mistake, an event over seventy years in the past and never spoken of since, not even between George and her.

Not a word.

She and George had been in the back of his car, not yet married, so young and so foolish and so head over heels in love with each other. Both just seventeen. And they'd gotten carried away. She'd let George go further than they'd ever gone before—in that steamy backseat, it felt so good, it felt so right—and before she knew it, what had been his finger became his… his thing. And it was inside of her.

She was shocked. Terrified. Going *all the way* wasn't the signal she'd meant to send. As far as they'd gone—and she'd assuredly let him go too far, they wouldn't go that far again until they were married—there were still limits.

She wasn't that kind of girl.

She told him to stop. Screamed it. But it was already too late. He'd lasted two, maybe three seconds inside of her. It had been his first time going this far, too. And he'd been done before she even realized what was happening. Before she could stop him.

Two or three seconds that changed their lives.

Filled with guilt and terror, they waited in the weeks and days to come for her to get her period. Never, of course, actually using that term. It was, after all, only a few years after World War II, a time of euphemisms and shame. With a fearful, shame-filled shake of the head in a dusty school hallway, she let George know that she was one day late.. then two days… then three. It became a week and then two, and then they both knew with a sickening knowledge in their guts that it was never going to come.

It had taken only that one time. That one shameful time. How could she have allowed it? She cried her eyes out, asking the question. How? She'd never been that kind of girl. She barely even knew the biology of it all.

So blissfully ignorant and innocent. But innocent no more.

Her life was over. And a bit of his was, too. They both came from respectable families. Respectable girls didn't get pregnant out of wedlock. Respectable boys, most of them, at least, didn't get such girls pregnant.

Those two or three seconds would ruin her. Her family would disown her in shame. Send her away or perhaps throw her to the wolves on the streets. She would cease to be a person in their eyes and all of polite society.

With *Roe v. Wade* still decades in the future, she resorted to the only option available. A butcher who left her barren, unable to ever have children. Lucky to be alive.

George stayed by her side and eventually married her, loyal when so many boys would have discarded her like weeks-old trash. He was a good man.

But no kids.

She had wanted children so badly. A family of five or six of them, running about a backyard with a thick lawn and hedges about the house, screeching their delight at whatever game they were playing, climbing trees, skinning knees, growing up so fast until soon they'd be having children of their own and she'd be a grandmother. By now, a great-grandmother. Or possibly even a great-great grandmother.

That was the way she'd always thought it should be. To

be denied it had been such a harsh, cruel penalty for her brief sin. If she thought about it long enough, even today, it tore her heart out, even if she supposed she ought to be grateful the butcher didn't kill her.

She and George never discussed it. It was a verboten topic. Their grief and guilt, shared but unspoken. Their marriage, a pact of loyalty but only a sliver of the joy that could have been theirs.

The Mistake, those two or three seconds, colored everything. Robbed them of so much.

And so when the *Roe v. Wade* ruling was announced, she had rejoiced, knowing that while it came too late for her —her womb and her life could not be repaired—it would protect young women like her, who made mistakes lasting only seconds or minutes, but would otherwise be given cruel penalties that lasted a lifetime.

Or a penalty of death.

She'd never spoken aloud of just why *Roe v. Wade* was so important to her. Her secret had been locked up tightly deep inside her heart.

Until now.

Deena stared at her. "What do you mean, girls like you?"

The Amazing RBG composed herself. She thrust her shoulders back and stuck out her jaw.

"You'll tell no one of what I just said. No one! Any clerk who violates confidence is signing her own career death warrant. Do you understand me?"

Deena sighed deeply and nodded.

"And so help me," the Amazing RBG said, "if you even mention this again, even just to me, I'll *habeas* your *corpus*!"

The hint of a smile poked through Deena's sad eyes.

The Amazing RBG shook her head, unable to fathom what Deena found amusing in such a grave subject.

<hr>

A WEEK LATER, a snot-nosed doctor barely old enough to wipe his own ass told the Amazing RBG of the cancer diagnosis. Treatable with chemo and radiation, but he wasn't sure her body was up to it. At her advanced age—

"Set up the chemo!" the Amazing RBG said. She nodded to Deena, sitting in the chair next to her in the doctor's compact office. "I ain't dead yet!"

The doctor, hands clasped, sitting behind a large black desk, clad all in white and good-looking with a full head of jet black hair straight out of a soap opera, tried to explain that he hadn't meant to convey that she was anywhere near death. Not at all. Just that on the cusp of age ninety, the body had a more difficult time—

"Did you vote for the Nazi?" she asked.

"Excuse me?" he asked, eyes wide in surprise.

"You support him, don't you?" the Amazing RBG said. "If you ain't a one-percenter, I don't know who is. A guy like you probably owns three mansions, four Maseratis, a trophy wife, and a mistress on the side. You just love that truckload of cash the Nazi gave you with that tax break."

"My political leanings are not—"

"I knew it!" the Amazing RBG exclaimed.

Deena took her hand and patted it, then said to the doctor, "Over the past several months, Mildred has become, shall we say, considerably more *forceful* in stating her opinions."

"You don't say," the young doctor said with a barely suppressed smirk. "I hadn't noticed."

"My opinions are my life now!" the Amazing RBG said. She pointed to the smartass doctor. "And I'm rendering the opinion that you are... *one of them*!"

She grabbed Deena's hand, stood, wobbled for a moment, and said, "Get me another quack."

And they were out of there.

Quack number two and quack number three, however, said the same thing.

Outlasting the monster had just become more difficult.

DAYS LATER, the Amazing RBG had forgotten the whole episode. She sat at the desk in her office, the goddamned place still smelling of urine. What the hell was wrong with facilities management in this place?

And what the hell did Deena's research on *Johansson v. District of Columbia* mean? If the Amazing RBG didn't know better, she'd think it was just some article copied from the *Boston Globe*. It had nothing to do with the case or with whoever this Johansson guy was. It simply talked about the latest changes in the District of Columbia's crime rate.

The Amazing RBG hadn't actually read the case itself. She'd tried but couldn't make one bit of sense out of it. Which was why she needed Deena to cover for her. That's what a good clerk did for a justice who was... struggling.

Hell, when Rehnquist couldn't put a coherent sentence together because of the pain meds he was on, his clerk covered for him. At least that's what George had told her years ago. The clerk made Rehnquist look good and sooner than you could say *caveat emptor*, Rehnquist had been elevated to Chief Justice.

Now *that* was a clerk!

Maybe that's what Deena was trying to do with *Johansson v. District of Columbia*, but it didn't it sure didn't seem it. The whole thing reeked of incompetence, plain and simple. The Amazing RBG sipped her coffee, by now only lukewarm. She shook her head ruefully. She hoped she wouldn't have to fire Deena. She'd come to like her in a certain sort of way.

Even if Deena was a godawful clerk.

On this day, she arrived late. That had *never* happened before. Deena might not know *Johansson v. District of Columbia* from her the hole in her backside, but she was always on time.

Never late.

A fearful look covered her face. "There's something you need to see." She swallowed hard. "Mrs. Hodges."

Mrs. Hodges?

A lightning bolt shot up and down the Amazing RBG's spine. It had been a long time since she'd heard that name. Oh, she'd had to fill it in on some paperwork here and there —one didn't have to be a Supreme Court justice to know you can't sign a legal document or even a credit card charge with "the Amazing RBG"—but Deena hadn't dared called her the H word for a very, very long time.

Until now.

But before the Amazing RBG could ream her clerk a new one, Deena gently placed the *Boston Globe* on the desk. She looked ready to cry. The front page headline screamed:

SUPREME COURT JUSTICE RACHEL BANSFIELD GRIFFIN SUFFERS FATAL HEART ATTACK

The Amazing RBG jerked back in her seat as if she'd been slapped. She shook her head, trying to clear the cobwebs.

Rachel Bansfield Griffin—*she!*—had died?

But how could that be? *I'm still here. Holding on until the monster leaves the White House.*

From somewhere that felt far, far away, Deena said softly, "Are you alright? If you'd like, I can turn on CNN."

The Amazing RBG felt her heart hammer wildly out of control.

She had to calm herself or else she really would have a fatal heart attack. Just like the newspaper said. And then the monster would win. He'd wipe out everything she had worked so hard for, everything that meant so much to her.

Including maybe even *Roe v. Wade*.

The Amazing RBG, who wasn't feeling very amazing at all, took a deep breath. Then another. And another.

You've got to hold on. Don't let the monster win.

Though it was probably just seconds, it felt like minutes —hours!—before her pulse slowed from its terrifying jack-hammer pace to a mere fast, hard pounding.

And then... just...

... thump, thump, thump.

Its normal rhythm.

She was still here. No matter what the newspapers might say. No matter what the TV stations might show. She was still here!

The Amazing RBG. Alive and kicking.

The thought occurred to her that it might even be fun to watch Fox News gleefully proclaim her death when the truth was—

I'm still here, you fuckers!

The Amazing RBG grinned wildly. Perhaps the body of Rachel Bansfield Griffin had died, but *she* was still here.

How could that be? She wasn't sure. But she knew she was still here.

Maybe she was one of the undead, she finally realized. She'd never believed in that nonsense, but maybe she was.

The Amazing RBG. A zombie!

She'd visit the White House. Gleefully show herself to the monster and announce he couldn't replace her on the court now. And as he stared at her in horror, she'd tell the bastard that she wouldn't feast on his brains.

Because he didn't have any!

The Amazing RBG howled with laughter. It rolled over her, over and over. A joy more pure and profound than one she'd ever known. She'd outlast them all.

Oh, to see the look on his face!

"Are you okay?" Deena asked gently. "Should I call for the doctor?"

"I've never been better!" the Amazing RBG proclaimed, tears of joy streaming down her face.

She'd beaten the monster! She'd won!

But her clerk looked terrified. So the Amazing RBG composed herself.

"Don't worry, Deena. I won't eat your brains." The Amazing RBG smiled. "Although I'm sure they'd be very tasty."

ONE-NIGHT STANDS FOR LOVE AND GLORY

INTRODUCTION TO "ONE-NIGHT STANDS FOR LOVE AND GLORY"

I rarely write science fiction. So it's no surprise that this is the only SF story in this collection. Yet would you care to guess which of my stories has been reprinted more than all others?

Yup. "One-Night Stands for Love and Glory." This will be the sixth time it appears in print. Go figure.

I wrote it back when traditional publishing was falling apart in early 2010. (Since then, it's become easier to track when traditional publishing *isn't* falling apart.) The story was for a *possible* themed anthology Denise Little *hoped* to edit for Tekno Books. I say *possible* and *hoped* because of that whole "traditional publishing falling apart" thing. At the time, Tekno Books packaged projects like unique anthologies for major publishers and after the project sold, took its slice of the profits. A win for all concerned: writers, Tekno, and the publishers. However, unlike two years earlier when Denise's two anthologies had already sold to DAW, Denise had not yet been able to place this one. And as it turned out, she never was able to place it. (See "publishing falling apart.")

At the time, though, I was willing to gamble on *possible*. No matter what, I'd learn more about writing, and Denise had already earned placement in my personal Hall of Fame when she bought my stories "Back to the Garden" and "Beloved" for those aforementioned DAW books. Those were my first two professional sales. I'll always remember my euphoria at seeing those books at the local bookstore.

I... was... a... real... writer. It boggled my mind.

So gambling on *possible* for Denise was a no-brainer. The lesson since learned, I suppose, is that you never bet financially on traditional publishing. But you always bet on learning. That part of the bet has always paid off for me.

It took another three years before "One-Night Stands for Love and Glory" sold to *Fiction River*, a new anthology series at the time that had hit the ground running and was now on its eighth volume, this one, *Fiction River: Universe Between*. "One-Night Stands" was a perfect fit for that theme and marked my sixteenth sale. Hey, maybe I could do this writing thing after all.

The story then *kept* selling.

Two years later, *Fiction River* introduced a reprint offshoot, *Fiction River Presents,* and included "One-Night Stands for Love and Glory." My first reprint ever! Yay! Three years after that, Dean Wesley Smith, to my great delight, selected it for *Pulphouse Fiction Magazine*, a legendary magazine from the nineties resuscitated after a twenty-one year hiatus. Then another two years later, Dean reprinted it in *Twisted Robots, Oh, My!: Stories from Pulphouse Fiction Magazine.*

Wow! You know a story has hit its mark when it not only gets published in two of your favorite magazines, but then *both* magazines reprint it.

Six years ago, it came time to assemble my first short story collection, *Shimmers and Laughs: Eight Wildly Hilarious Tales*. Featuring "One-Night Stands for Love and Glory" was another a no-brainer. (I'm surprisingly good at no-brainers, perhaps due to a lifetime of practice.) I placed it in the time-honored position of the collection's final story, the one that when the reader sets the book down convinces her to buy your next one.

Which brings us to this volume and yet another no-brainer. While this story was an automatic inclusion in that earlier Humor collection and thus would be a "repeat," it also ranks among my most poignant stories about aging. It left me with no choice but to include it.

I hope "One-Night Stands for Love and Glory" touches your funny bone, your heart, and your soul.

ONE-NIGHT STANDS FOR LOVE
AND GLORY

$\mathcal{N}$ow where was I?

Oh, yes, of course. The introduction. How silly of me.

Welcome to the show, ladies and gentlemen. What a great crowd we have here in the . . . the, um . . . what is the name of this place?

Yes! Yes, thank you. The People's Auditorium. Of course. I knew that. I was just testing you, ha ha.

It's a delight to be here. It's been a long time since I performed under a straw thatch roof. And the gaps in the logs that make up these walls provide such wonderful venti-lation. What a good thing that is, I can tell most of you were working really hard in the fields today. Smells like some of you might even have been spreading manure, ha ha.

I'm just joking. You're a great audience. Give yourself a hand!

Get on with the show?

Ah, yes. A splendid idea. Splendid!

There's just one problem. As you may have surmised, I'm stalling. I tell you that in a spirit of forthright openness.

No, there's no reason for you to leave. And there are positively no refunds! Of course not, the show is free, ha ha.

Please be patient. I'm experiencing technical difficulties. My AI is not responding.

Yes, a chip implant translates my words into your local dialect, but I need Artie, my AI, to translate them even further into your culture. Most jokes make no sense without the correct cultural grounding. I really can't start without him.

Artie?

Folks, please sit down. This is temporary, I assure you. He'll be with us momentarily.

One Universal Credit to everyone who stays for the entire show! You have my word on it. Your patience will be rewarded.

Hey, there's no need to throw anything.

Oooh. That one was juicy. Really now! That was quite unnecessary.

Oh my, that one was rotten.

Two credits to everyone who stays! Without, of course, throwing either soft rotten objects or very hard ones.

Ah, that's more like it. You are a fine and cultured audience.

Artie? Artieeeeeee?

Let me demonstrate, folks why I can't perform without my AI. You might even find this enlightening.

As the old phrase goes, please stand by.

You're sitting down.

Why are you still sitting down? This is where I'm

supposed to tell you that "Please stand by" is only a phrase, a figure of speech, not meant to be taken literally. A phrase that Artie would have translated into one that you understood.

But you did understand. How did you do that?

Artie? You're here? What do you mean you've been here all along?

Ah, well, let's get on with the show then.

Folks, I flew in just last night and boy, are my arms tired.

I'm glad that one is over. I thought the crowd was going to lynch me there for a while. But they came around after a while, the bunch of dumb hicks. Not all the way, but enough for me to see their front teeth, all two or three of them, as they laughed. The front row looked like a picket fence.

At least a few of the jokes scored. Not as many as in the old days when Artie was in his prime, but enough.

Now where was I? What was I saying?

Oh yes, Artie.

He's slipping, bit by bit, byte by byte. It's sad, not just for him but for me, too, because I can't make it without him. When he's gone—gone for good, I mean, not just gone for a while like now—I'll be nothing.

Of course, I'm pretty close to nothing even with him. If I were *something*, I'd be in one of the galactic centers, where all the great comic talents showcase their brilliance. I tried that for a time, crashed and burned, so now I play these two-bit halls out here in the Great In-Between, where habitable planets are few and far between and comic brilliance can't be found.

On Old Earth, they said of New York City that if you could make it there, you could make it anywhere. Out here in the cosmic boonies, we say that if you *can't* make it anywhere, you try the Great In-Between.

That's my joke, by the way. I steal most of my material, but that's an Earl Weatherbee original. If you liked it, come to my next show and drop a Universal Credit in the hat on your way out.

I could get another AI, of course, but Artie and I have been working together so long—over fifty years—I could never adjust. And if I could, I doubt it would be worth it. No other AI could match his old brilliance. Your average AI can make the translation when there's a one-to-one match in the cultures. But Artie, before he started this slide, could pull off even the most impossible of matches.

Don't believe me?

Well, let me tell you about the joke that started it all and you can be the judge.

WHEN I WAS TWELVE, my best friend, Jimmy Chiasson, and I were Old Earth history buffs. These days, I can take it or leave it but back then both of us were addicted. We loved to go into the archives and relive Old Earth history, playing all sorts of strange recordings, things they called "movies" and "TV shows" back then.

Jimmy and I watched and listened to them all, but for one brief stretch we liked the Lone Ranger TV show best of all. We got a chill up and down our spines just hearing the theme music. It went like this: *tada-dum, tada-dum, tada-dum-dum-dum. Tada-dum, tada-dum, tada-dum-dum-dum.*

That theme song gave birth to my first joke ever and sent me on to a life of one-night stands. I'm almost certain I made it up myself—who could I have stolen it from?—but you know how it is with us low-rent comics; we've stolen so many jokes, we can't recall what's really our own and what's somebody else's bastard child.

Now where was I? Bastard child . . . um, oh yeah. Where it all started. Sorry. If I didn't know better, I'd think that whatever Artie has is catchy and I've lost a few of my own marbles. But that's ludicrous. I know I've still got it.

Anyways, back then I was as horny as any other boy my age, so one time, for some reason I'll never understand, I happened to think of naked women at the same time the Lone Ranger theme song came on.

Tada-dum, tada-dum, tada-dum-dum-dum.

I had a burst of comic inspiration. I paused the recording and turned to Jimmy.

"If you had a room of a hundred naked women," I said, catching his attention right away. "And they all laid down on the floor, one face up and then the next face down, one face up, and the next face down . . . how would that be like the Lone Ranger?"

Jimmy grinned. "I don't know."

"*Titty-bum, titty-bum, titty-bum-bum-bum.*"

Jimmy howled with laughter. He laughed so hard he had to hold his sides.

I was hooked. I knew what I wanted to do with my life.

What I *had* to do for the rest of my life. I had to make people laugh like that every day.

Some days I want to damn Jimmy's soul to Hell for that laughter, for those tears that trickled down the sides of his face. If he'd only given me a frown and called me a stupid pervert, he'd have spared me the life I've lived, hopping about in the Great In-Between, having to pay people not to leave my shows.

I can't even say that it's a living. Not that I need one. My parents left me a trust fund so huge not even I could possibly squander it. I get my gigs only by agreeing to appear without compensation, paying all my own interstellar expenses.

Which means I'm the saddest of all artists. I don't do it for the money. I do it for the love. And you know what that means.

I'm not good enough for anyone to pay me.

SO WHERE WAS I?

Oh, yeah. Artie losing it.

No, that isn't right.

Where the Hell was I?

Oh yeah, Artie's old brilliance and the Lone Ranger joke. That's it.

You see, that's about as cultural as any joke you're ever going to hear. It doesn't make any sense unless you know the Lone Ranger theme song. And what percentage of the human population, especially out here in the galactic boondocks, knows that? Virtually zero. Plus, the local people need to have words in their dialect for their titties and bums that match the words you'd use for the rhythms of that music.

The odds are astronomical.

And yet, I include that joke in every show. It's my signature joke in fact, and somehow Artie's been able to translate it every time and it always brings down the house.

Well, maybe it doesn't bring down the house. I don't ever really *bring down the house*. But the joke works. Every time. One of the best in my repertoire.

Until recently, of course. Until Artie began to drop a few bits here and there. Then a few more.

Now, as a team we're in crisis mode. He acts as though it's me that's messing up. He can't accept the fact that I'm sharp as ever and it's him that's losing it and losing it fast.

It's so sad.

The denial must be an AI thing.

IT GOT WORSE on the next planet. But it turned out great in its own way.

Artie bombed, leaving me dying up there on stage.

Dying, I tell you.

I went five minutes without a laugh and then ten. I had expected the hillbilly audience of about five hundred to be easy picking, as willing as a horny ninety-year-old man to take whatever entertainment it could get.

But by the fifteen-minute mark, the frozen smiles were long gone. I'd coaxed not a single laugh out of any of them. Men and women looked at each other confused. A man in the front row turned to what I assume was his wife and mouthed the words, "This is comedy?"

I knew then that Artie, who'd been slipping, had lost it for good. My material was the same as always, but Artie's translations were missing the mark.

As people shifted uncomfortably in their seats, long past the twenty-minute mark, I was rescued only in the most bizarre and humiliating of ways.

Suddenly, a peach-faced young man in the very middle of the audience stood up and yelled, "He's a Kaufmanite!" He spread his arms wide and grinned broadly. "Like the comedian on Old Earth. He's *trying* to be bad! That's what's so funny!"

And he howled with laughter.

As bad as the twenty minutes of dead silence had been, this was worse. Far worse. It was a mocking slap in the face.

But a few people around him began to titter and then as he continued to roar and slap his leg, so did they. Couples looked at each other, first confused and then with dawning amusement. The laughter became infectious, spreading out from the young man like ripples in the water after a stone has been tossed into it.

Soon the entire auditorium was howling and slapping their legs. Some of them in the front row were laughing so hard, they were crying.

When they broke into thunderous applause, I almost said, "I'm not done, I've got lots more where that came from."

But I thought better of it.

I spread my arms wide and bowed.

"You're too kind," I mouthed to them. I blew them kisses. As the cheering reached its crescendo, I bowed again.

And walked off the stage to the first standing ovation of my career.

I SHOULD HAVE CALLED it quits right then. Gone out on a high note. A standing ovation after the last performance of my career! Yes, the truth would have mocked me. The laughter and applause for all the wrong reasons would have haunted my days and nights.

But I might have become a legend out here in the Great In-Between. The two-bit comic with a brief flash of brilliance, showing his true genius in that one singular bravura performance. Knowing he could never duplicate it, he retired atop the very peak of the comic mountaintop. The most romantic of all artistic legends short of also blowing my brains out.

Legends, after all, are created easily out here in the galactic boonies because the fabric they require is so scarce and the hunger for them is so fierce.

That outcome might have been the funniest joke of all, even funnier than the one about the Lone Ranger.

Earl Weatherbee, legendary comic.

A *real* knee-slapper.

But I'm a creature of habit. Moving from planet to planet and solar system to solar system is what I do. Besides, I'd have probably blabbed the truth on my deathbed and ruined the romantic legend anyway.

So I moved on to the next one-night stand and the one

after that and eventually took the stage on a planet with two rival humanoid races, one with traditional arms and legs, the Bipeds, and the other with eight tentacled appendages, the Octoids.

An aisle ran through the middle of the auditorium—there was not a single center seat—and the two races sat on their respective sides. Artie couldn't reach out to two such contradictory cultures, even though he'd mastered even that impossible task in his prime. That feat was beyond him now.

So, of course, I bombed.

He bombed, but *I* was the one left standing in front of the crowd with an embarrassed grin on my face. Undressed, in a manner of speaking.

Less than halfway through the show, the crowds streamed to their respective exits, members of both races equally unwilling to subject themselves to the performance even when offered five Universal Credits apiece.

I WAITED until I was back in the hotel room with its rusted sink, leaky faucet, and squeaking bed. Damp moldy smells filled my nostrils. The bitter, almost sour aftertaste of the local malt beverage clung to my palate.

I'd been in this place, or places like it, my entire adult life. But no more.

"Artie, we have to talk," I said out loud.

You don't have to shout, he replied.

"I'm not shouting."

It feels like it.

For the longest time, we'd communicated almost subconsciously. I'd *thought* the words and he'd received them, replying in kind. But words of this import— words of beginnings, words of endings—demanded more.

"I need to say this out loud. For me, if not for you."

Knock yourself out.

"I don't know if you've noticed the audience reactions lately."

How could I not? I may not be organic, but your senses are mine.

I nodded. "We've been dying lately."

We?

Relief washed over me. Artie knew and was accepting the blame. I wouldn't have to spell it out for him. Yet with that relief came a sudden onrushing wave of sadness.

Could there be a more tragic plight than that of a once brilliant consciousness, whether organic or AI, reduced first to mediocrity and then to a barely aware feeble-mindedness?

"I'm so very sorry."

You're doing the best you can.

"I'll never trade you—" I stopped. "What did you just say?"

Don't feel badly. I know you're trying as hard as you can.

"But . . ." I cocked my head. "I'm not the problem."

Who is?

Silence hung in the air for what felt like forever.

"You don't think . . ."

You can't possibly think—

"I'm telling the same jokes as always."

Are you?

"Of course. I haven't written or stolen a new joke in years."

But you aren't telling them anymore. Most of the time you're just babbling gibberish. It's untranslatable. I love a challenge, but I can't turn random babbling into a local joke. I can only turn it into locally understood random babbling. You're giving me nothing to work with.

"Random babbling? You call my act random babbling?"

That's what it is. Babbling about the cutie in row seven or the foul smell of the air or how you hate Jimmy Chiasson.

"I said that?"

Check the diagnostic logs. They'll show your input and my output.

My head felt light. The hotel room with its water-stained walls and dank smells spun all about me. "Garbage in, garbage out?"

You said it, not me. Or you tell the same joke in the same performance.

"I do not!"

Three times tonight. Would you like me to tell you which ones?

I shook my head, unable to speak.

Or you get halfway through a joke, then forget the punch line. You stand there and I can't help you. You just start it all over again. Sometimes you get stuck in a loop like that, repeating the first half over and over.

"I do?"

The worst one tonight lasted over five minutes.

"Five minutes?"

I suddenly recalled all the times I'd stood before a full

auditorium, unable to remember why I was there. A cold chill crept up and down my spine.

"I'm losing it . . . aren't I?"

Some things are still clear for you. You've never forgotten the Lone Ranger joke. But I have to be honest . . . . Yes, you're losing it. I'm so very sorry.

My heart thudded and my palms felt moist. "Can't you . . . I mean, you know my material by heart, why don't you fix it when I start . . . when I start losing it?"

You don't know the answer? I thought sure you would remember that.

"The answer to what?"

To why I can't override you.

"Override me when?"

Do you see what I mean?

"No, I don't see." I blinked my eyes and licked my lips. "What were we talking about?"

About me overriding you.

"I forbid it! I'm the maestro. You are but the instrument!"

Exactly.

"Exactly what?"

We were talking about your fugues.

"We were? What fugues?"

And how I'm powerless to help you when they happen on stage.

"You are?"

They're happening almost all the time now, but you've forbidden me to help.

Clouds parted within my mind.

"You're serious? I've really lost it?"

I'm afraid so. It's getting worse and worse.

"Lost and gone forever? Dreadful sorry, Clementine?"

Dreadful sorry, Earl.

"This is awful. What will I do? What will *you* do?"

Don't worry. I won't leave you. I'll stay with you, no matter what.

"Until . . . until the very . . ."

I couldn't speak that last word.

Yes.

"You shouldn't."

Try to stop me.

I thought of all our years together. Good times. Bad times. I'd never expected it to end like this.

"I don't want to stop performing." I bowed my head. "But if I'm just humiliating myself . . ."

Let me help. I know the material. When you space out, I'll take over. We'll be co-maestros.

"You think so?"

You could maybe even try some new material. I've thought up some for you.

"Use your material?"

Only if you want to.

AT OUR NEXT SHOW, we killed them. The audience, I mean. Perhaps a modest success by inner galactic standards, but a rip-roaring smash out here in the Great In-Between.

Artie's new material about having sex with an Octoid woman got some of the biggest laughs.

Women with tentacles, woo-ee, they'll grab your scrawny

ass, never let go, and have six limbs left over for everything else!

For the first time in decades, I found myself laughing. Not fake stage laughter. But really laughing.

"Knock 'em dead, Artie," I whispered. "Knock 'em dead."

HE'S DOING MORE and more of each show. Not that Artie's taking over or anything like that. Just that my blank spots are becoming more and more frequent. I'm leaning more and more heavily on him all the time. We both know the old Earl Weatherbee isn't coming back.

You wouldn't believe how long I had to wait just to clearly tell you these few words.

But I'm not going to quit. Making people laugh is my life. It's who I am; it's what I do. If I need a little help—or a lot of help—so what?

It doesn't matter which one of us is telling the jokes, does it? Who cares? Artie and me, we're a team. I've hopped on his back and he's carrying me home. It's a nice back. A hell of a back.

And if he's all I have as the last of my flickering lights go out...well, that's all right with me.

SULLY AND THE GEEZER

INTRODUCTION TO "SULLY AND THE GEEZER"

I've appeared in almost every issue of *Mystery, Crime, and Mayhem* since the magazine first began publishing in 2020. I'm one member of a "syndicate" of professional writers who agree to submit stories for at least half the issues.

So when I saw there would be a themed issue of BOLO, the standard police acronym for Be On the Lookout, I sat down at my writing desk determined to write a story but unsure where that topic would lead me. Ten years earlier, I would have written a completely different story from "Sully and the Geezer," one having *nothing* to do with aging. It simply wasn't on my radar. But by 2020, when this story was written, old age and its issues filled my radar screen.

I didn't set out that day to write about my new obsession. After all, aging and a police force's BOLO make for an unnatural pairing. Not exactly peanut butter and jelly, bagels and cream cheese, or pancakes and maple syrup. This odd couple of topics would not make my job easy. Then, for reasons known only to my mischievous creative subconscious, I found myself tossing in another new passion of mine, triathlons. Because two near mutually exclusive concerns weren't enough. I had to go for the hat trick.

How were those three topics possibly going to fit together? Damned if I knew. I just followed the classic, time-honored writer's recipe.

Cram whatever you can find into your creative blender, crank up its settings to the max, and ignore the billowing clouds of ominous, black smoke filling the room. Season to taste. Serve piping hot.

SULLY AND THE GEEZER

7:30 p.m.
January 9

Sully couldn't believe what he was hearing from the Lieutenant, a gray-haired, burly man in his fifties, seated at his desk while Sully and his evening watch partner, Dez, stood just inside the closed office door. Dez, short for Desmond Tutu Jackson, was ten years Sully's junior, but at six-one, one hundred ninety-five pounds had Sully by two inches, ten pounds, and by a billion miles in the looks department. Denzel Washington to Sully's somewhat taller version of Danny DeVito. They both wore the dark suits and ties befitting their detective status, but Dez's was impeccably tailored and fit him like a glove while Sully's looked perpetually rumpled.

"You gotta be shitting me, Loot." Sully spread his hands wide, palms up, in the time-honored gesture that asked what-the-hell. "You want us to drop everything else for this? I get it when the Missing Persons case is a sixteen-year-old girl who's been abducted. But an eighty-five-year-old geezer who wandered off from his fucking nursing home? Are you kidding me?"

The Lieutenant pursed his lips. He didn't look particularly pleased either. "At least make an attempt to use the proper words. Sunshine Acres is not a nursing home; it's one of the finest retirement facilities in Massachusetts. And geezer is hardly appropriate either. We do not use words here that are racist, sexist, ageist, homophobic, transphobic, or—"

"Yeah, yeah, I read the manual," Sully said.

The Lieutenant fixed him with an icy glare. "So as I was saying, Frank Bennett isn't a geezer. He's a valued citizen like everyone else."

"Apparently a lot *more* valued than everyone else," Sully said.

"In other words, a rich, white dude," Dez said, and raised his eyebrows, his version of spiking the football after a verbal touchdown.

"Don't give me that shit, Dez," the Lieutenant said, his face flushing. "This has nothing to do with race." But he looked away as he handed full-page photos of the missing person, Frank Bennett, to the two detectives. "We put out a BOLO as soon as the disappearance was reported just after noontime, and circulated photos for all the uniforms on evening watch. So far, no luck."

Dez held the photo out for Sully to see even though he had one of his own. "Sure looks white to me."

The Lieutenant ignored the comment. "Temperatures

are dropping fast tonight. After midnight, it's going to be in the single digits with wind chill below zero. Weather like that will kill the old man if he's outdoors. So we need to escalate.

"Problem is, he has dementia. Can remember his own name, but not much more. Can't recognize family members other than his wife, and there's some doubt about whether he's been faking that, too. Gets lost trying to find his own apartment after eating at a dining facility he's been going to for over five years."

Sully caught a sideways glance from Dez, who was clenching and unclenching his jaw. Sully recognized the unspoken request to keep Dez from saying something he'd regret.

Saying shit he lived to regret was Sully's role.

"Loot, we got that," Sully said. "We're concerned about the guy. But why can't the uniforms take care of this? You've got the BOLO out. They've got the photos. Not to be a dick, but you want us to drop everything for a fucking dementia case who can't even make it back from a dining hall to his apartment? Dez is right. We ain't doing this if it's an old black guy in the projects. Even one who still has all his marbles."

Left unsaid was the turmoil in the police department of this tough, gritty city known as "Lynn, Lynn, City of Sin." After George Floyd's murder and the nationwide protests that ensued, reforms had been proposed and implemented, some mere superficial publicity stunts but others with substance for which the jury was still out. This case seemed to make a lie of it all. The white guy was special. Sully didn't need to be black to smell the stench of it.

Silence hung heavy in the air.

The Lieutenant glared at both of them, then slowly rose from his seat, put both hands on his desk, and leaned forward.

"Enough out of both of you," he said. "There are special circumstances here, and I'll explain them to you in just a second. After I do, I want to hear only two words out of you two assholes and those words will be, 'Yes, Sir!' Do you fucking understand me?"

Sully took a sideways glance at Dez. They both nodded.

The Lieutenant took a long, noisy inhalation through his flared nostrils. His eyes moved from Sully to Dez and back, seeming to try to burn holes in both their eyeballs.

"*One of you* is going to be dedicated to finding Frank Bennett, and it damned well better be alive. The other will stick with your current caseload. If, by chance, one man isn't enough to handle an unarmed eighty-five-year-old... *geezer*"—the Lieutenant looked pointedly at Sully—"your partner is a phone call away."

Sully resisted the urge to look triumphantly at Dez. Sully didn't like to pull rank. They were partners. But if there was a shit job to do, it was a relief to a veteran like himself that the junior member of the team got stuck with it.

Besides, Sully felt *this close* to a breakthrough in one of their cases. There was some detail he was overlooking. He could smell it. And he'd figure it out, with luck before Dez got the geezer back to the old folk's home.

"Dez, you stick with the current caseload," the Lieutenant said. "Sully, find the old man."

Sully blinked. Had he heard that wrong? He must have. But Dez was grinning broadly.

"Loot, why me?" Sully asked.

For the first time, the Lieutenant smiled.

"First, because you're an insubordinate asshole, and you're on my shit list. In fact, you're on my *permanent* shit list. Second, if you fuck this up and the mayor wants someone's head on a platter, I'd rather it be yours."

Sully stared in amazement at Dez. "Can you believe this?"

Dez couldn't have wiped the shit-eating grin off his face with a soapy dishcloth and two towels. "Sorry, partner."

Sully stared back at the Lieutenant. "You're serious?"

The Lieutenant nodded, but then the smile was gone.

"The Missing Person isn't just any dementia case," he said. "He's the mayor's father-in-law."

8:00 p.m.

SULLY WAS STILL SWEARING up a storm as he pulled the Crown Vic up to the Sunshine Acres guardhouse, brightly lit in the evening darkness. This case was the equivalent of a two-foot putt in golf. You could only fuck it up. If you succeeded, you were supposed to. It was easy. Trivial. No credit for that. But all hell would break lose if you didn't. Yet another shitstorm.

Right up his fucking alley.

Sully shook his head in disbelief. The mayor's fucking father-in-law. Shit on a shingle.

Freezing cold air blew in his face as Sully opened the Crown Vic's window to show his badge to the guard, a pudgy, middle-aged man dressed like a uniformed cop, including a black, hard-billed cap covering salt-and-pepper, curly hair. He had all but the badge, but was acting like he had that too, plus a captain's stripes.

He took his grand old time scribbling Sully's name and the Crown Vic's license plate on a sheet on his clipboard. "Reason for the visit?"

"Police business," Sully said, knowing he could be more cooperative, maybe even should be more cooperative, but he was just not... in... the... fucking... mood. He had a BOLO out, but it wasn't for Frank Bennett. Sully's permanent BOLO was for assholes. And this pretentious prick was a dead ringer.

The pretentious prick cocked his head. "Sorry, sir, but I have to ask this question. Who are you here to see?"

"I'm here on official police business and I'll see whoever the fuck I want to see," Sully said. "Now you can either open that candy-ass gate"—he pointed to the horizontal, two-inch-wide piece of plastic that swung up and down, a pathetic excuse for a gate that he could snap in half with his dick if he wanted to—"or I'll drive right through it and you can spend the rest of the night picking up the pieces. I don't really care one way or another."

The prick, not quite so pretentious now, swallowed hard, as if Sully had crammed the clipboard halfway down his throat. "Yes, sir," the guard said, nodding. "Main entrance to the East buildings is off to your right." He pointed to two large, connected brick buildings, each of them about the length of a football field and six floors high.

Lights shone from most of the windows. "The West buildings are on your left." He handed Sully a license-plate sized parking pass for the dashboard.

Magically, the gate went up. Magically, Sully crumped the parking pass and tossed it on the passenger-side floor.

And to think, he mused, that some people said he had a bad attitude.

In retrospect, he realized he could have asked which building Frank Bennett lived in. That wouldn't exactly have been difficult detective work. But what the hell. The prick probably would have taken five minutes to look it up.

Sully guessed the East buildings, and of course, guessed wrong. A gray-haired woman at the front desk told him that Mr. Bennett lived in West 684, so Sully, freezing his nuts off, climbed back in the Crown Vic and headed to the other side of the major complex.

A lot of really old, really rich people.

And one of them a major pain in Sully's ass. There probably wasn't a single thing special about the guy. Except that he was the mayor's father-in-law, of course. Which put the bullseye squarely on Sully's forehead.

Sully tried to pump the woman at the front desk just inside the West main entrance for possible information, but got nowhere. She was about forty, slender, with brown hair cut short, and was as tight-lipped as a CIA agent. Other than insisting that Sully sign into her log book like any other visitor, she just replied robotically to every question. "Mr. Bennett is a wonderful man. I hope you find him soon."

After hearing how wonderful Frank Bennett was for the third fucking time, Sully gave up. In spite of himself, he asked for directions, and she pointed down the carpeted hallway to a bank of elevators, then told him to take a right and a left once he got to the sixth floor.

———

8:15 p.m.

EDITH BARRETT, the mayor's mother-in-law and wife of the missing Frank Barrett, answered the door on the second ring. Leaning heavily on a walker, she looked frail, almost emaciated, her rust red hair—an obvious dye job—pulled up in a bun. Her eyes were bloodshot, her bright red lipstick smudged at the corners of her mouth. She wore a black dress with a white-and-black striped blouse.

"I thought you'd never get here," she said, and looked about to burst into tears.

Taking the tiniest of steps behind her walker, she ushered Sully past a wall filled with rows of family photographs and into a spacious living room with a large picture window on the far wall, a tan sofa and coffee table on the left, and a television on the right.

She gestured to the sofa. "Have a seat. Can I get you something to drink?"

"Thanks, I'm fine," Sully said. "I'd rather look around, if you don't mind, Mrs. Bennett."

"Call me Edith."

"Edith, then." Sully wasn't usually much for small talk, but this was the wife of the missing man, and the mother-in-law of the mayor, to boot. Despite what the Lieutenant and half the squad thought, Sully wasn't totally without social graces. A good detective couldn't be a hard-ass all the time. Sully could be charming when he wanted to be. He just didn't want to be very often.

"I'm sorry for your situation," he said. "I'll do everything in my power to find your husband and bring him back here, safe and sound."

Edith Bennett nodded, and forced a smile. "I can't imagine where he is. It could be almost anywhere. I'm so worried."

Sully verified what little information he had, namely that Frank Bennett had disappeared just after noontime while Edith napped. The Bennetts' car, a six-year-old Lexus, was still parked in its assigned parking spot. And Frank Bennett hadn't used a computer in years, not since his mind had started to go, so there were no recent websites visited or Google searches to serve as leads.

Sully figured the old man couldn't have gone far. He hasn't taken the family car, and according to the preliminary investigation, no taxi, Uber, or other service had picked him up. How far could an eighty-five-year-old man go?

"Do you mind if I look around?" Sully asked again, not really caring whether she minded or not, but trying to be polite.

It was quite the apartment for a retirement home. Sunshine Acres living up to its reputation. Plush carpeting and drapes everywhere. A master bedroom with expensive-looking art on the back wall and a flat screen TV on the front. Two full bathrooms, one with an impressive vanity and large mirror just outside it. A kitchen with all the latest appliances and a fully stocked wine rack.

But what stopped Sully was the study and its wall of medals and trophies above a mahogany desk and chair. Hundreds of medals hung from hooks on mahogany racks. Above them, matching shelves held what had to be almost fifty trophies of sizes up to two feet high. The side walls held row after row of photographs of Frank Bennett in the middle of races—running or cycling or swimming—or crossing finish lines, arms uplifted in victory. Short and wiry, maybe five-eight and only a hundred forty pounds. Dark hair plastered to his scalp. To Sully's astonishment, many of the images showed a man only marginally younger than the BOLO photograph.

"Your husband was quite the athlete," Sully said to Edith Bennett, leaning on her walker just inside the open study door.

"Oh, yes," she said. "He ran the Boston marathon over forty times, winning his age group almost every time after he turned sixty. He even performed in Ironman triathlons until just a few years ago. Can you imagine that? Swim two and a half miles, cycle for a hundred and twelve, and then run a full marathon! And you have to finish in under eighteen hours."

Forget about dementia, Sully thought. You had to be mentally ill to do that shit.

"Did you say until just a few years ago?" Sully asked, sure he hadn't heard right even though many of the photographs backed up the contention. Wrinkled, weathered skin. The sagging muscle tone befitting his advanced age even in strong arms raised in victory.

"At the age of seventy-nine, he completed the Ironman triathlon in Lake Placid, one of the most difficult ones in the world," Edith said proudly. "He was the only one over seventy to finish the race. It was quite extraordinary." Pointing, she said, "That medal over there on the far right edge, the one with the bright red ribbon. That's the one he got for that race. It became one of Frank's favorites."

Instead of a medal, Sully thought, they should award a fucking straitjacket. Doing all that was crazy at any age. But at seventy-nine? Totally insane. It made his own bones ache. His idea of a tough workout was lifting an ice cold beer to his lips and then actually setting it down.

"He competed in the Kona world championships several times," Edith added, then sighed deeply. "It makes what's happened to his mind all the more tragic. His body is still willing, amazingly enough, but..." A distant look came to her eyes. "He'd go out for a run, but he couldn't find his way back because he couldn't remember where he lived. And he couldn't run with someone, because no one could keep up with him.

"I got calls all the time to pick him up. One time, he cycled all the way up to New Hampshire then had no idea where he was." She shrugged. "I was afraid for him, but he wouldn't listen. Got angry if I even suggested that he stop. So I'd be ready with my phone in my trembling hands, waiting for him to call.

"Until the day he forgot who to call." Edith stared at the carpeted floor. Tears pooled in her eyes. One leaked out and streamed down her face. Then another. Sully wanted to comfort her, but in a cold-hearted way, he needed to hear all this and didn't want to stop the words gushing out. "That day," Edith said, her voice shaking, "the call I got came from the police, not Frank. He was okay physically. He just didn't know who to call.

"He'd been holding it all together, just barely, teetering on the precipice, windmilling his arms, and then..." She looked at Sully and shook her head mournfully. "He went over the edge. Into the abyss."

Edith took a deep breath. Sully waited.

"So he had to be restricted to the gym here—which is truly exceptional—and the pool. We sold his bike, and instructed the guards at the front gate to turn him back if he went out for a run. Or if he tried to go out driving alone. He could only drive with me in the car.

"Frank didn't like it at first, and even snuck out a few times, going out through the back bushes instead of the front gate. I got a few calls. Not from him. From you people, the police." She nodded at Sully. "I had to come pick him up. He'd be so apologetic, so embarrassed, and swore he'd never do it again. But then I'd get another call.

"Pretty soon, though, he stopped. The last time might have been almost two years ago." Edith looked at Sully. "A lifetime ago." She shook her head. "Apparently, what was left of his mind realized he couldn't get out and make it back in on his own. And he hated the humiliation of you people having to figure out who he was and contacting me. So he stopped. Never did it again.

"Now, he runs the treadmill, rides the stationary bike, lifts weights, and swims laps in the pool. Like clockwork, an attendant comes to take Frank down there because he can't remember where it is even though he goes there every day. And then another attendant brings him back because he can't remember where his own apartment is.

It's all part of his daily routine now, like brushing his teeth.

"He was depressed for a while, stuck in the gym instead of getting outside. Who wouldn't be, running on a treadmill instead of those trails he loved so much? At first, he called the treadmill the *dreadmill*. But he got over it, and lately, he's been quite happy."

Sully's eyebrows shot up. "Happy? For how long?"

"Maybe the last month or so."

"Why do you think that is?"

Edith shrugged. "I have no idea. I guess I thought—I hoped—he had somehow come to peace with himself. With what he'd become. His mind had weakened to the point that it didn't care, or didn't even realize, that it didn't work very well anymore."

Sully waited, but Edith remained silent.

"Could it have been that this past month he was hatching a plan to escape again?" Sully asked. "He was happy because... he planned to get out of here?"

Edith Bennett's face turned ashen. "For good? Like he's in jail here with me? I would hope not."

"No, not that," Sully said quickly, feeling compassion for the poor woman. "I meant that he might have been planning to sneak out just for a run, like old times, nothing more. Could that be all this is?"

"It's possible," Edith said slowly. "But don't think so. It's been so long since he's tried anything like that. He's became so conditioned to sticking with his routine. Routine has become everything to him. He goes down to the gym even on his one rest day each week and just hangs out. Because that's what his schedule is.

"And he certainly couldn't manage planning something for a month. He might instinctively think of something and act on it, but his planning days ended a long time ago. He's just not capable of that kind of sustained, organized thought. For him, he starts every day, every hour, sometimes it feels like every minute, back at square one."

She tried to smile weakly, but failed. She looked down at her hands.

"Is there anything at all that changed this last month?" Sully asked. "Other than his suddenly positive mood? Anything that might have been linked to it? Anything at all?"

Edith sadly shook her head. "I have no idea. I'm sorry."

"Okay, one other thing," Sully said. "You mentioned trails. Were there specific trails your husband liked to run? Perhaps a nearby favorite one he might have gone to this time? To escape the *dreadmill*?"

"Well, I suppose so," Edith said. "But they were all clear across town. About a fifteen-minute drive, more if the traffic was bad. Frank would always drive over because he didn't like running through all that congestion and breathing all that car exhaust. He said it was bad for the lungs. So he'd drive over to Lynn Woods and run the trails there. But he didn't take the car today."

Lynn Woods was a park loaded with thirty miles of trails for hikers, horseback riders, and cyclists. Three times the size of New York City's Central Park, it contained a couple thousand acres of forests and reservoirs, not to mention a golf course and ball field just outside one set of gates. If that's where Frank Bennett was, it would be like trying to find a needle in a two-thousand-acre haystack.

But it was something.

"Any particular trails?" Sully asked.

"I think he liked them all," Edith said.

Great, Sully thought.

8:55 p.m.

WHILE TRYING to make a mad dash to the Sunshine Acres gym before it closed, Sully called Dez.

"Any chance I can get your help?" Sully said.

"Officer needs assistance? Eighty-five-year-old guy kicking your ass?"

Sully ignored the dig and Dez's warm chuckle. "The guy's a fitness nut. I mean, a freaking Superman. I think he might be in Lynn Woods. Maybe along one of the trails."

"Somewhere in Lynn Woods? Now? In pitch black darkness?"

"It's just a hunch," Sully admitted. "But yeah."

"So you got a *hunch* that this guy might be somewhere, *anywhere*, in all of Lynn Freaking Woods. And you want me to ignore the Lieutenant's *direct* order and come save your sorry ass? *Seriously?*"

"I take it that's a no," Sully said.

"You're gonna need a bigger boat."

9:00 p.m.

WITH DEZ'S use of their line for impossible tasks ringing in his ears, Sully got to the Sunshine Acres gym. A muscular, blond-haired man in his twenties was closing and locking the gym door, his winter jacket looped over one arm. A tight, dark blue T-shirt showcased his every muscle. Inside the gym's glass walls, darkness cloaked vague shapes of weight machines, free weights, stationary bikes, and treadmills.

Dreadmills.

"Excuse me," Sully said.

"I'm sorry, we're closed," the young man said, as he turned around. He frowned. "Do I know you?"

Sully *almost* said, "Do I look like I'm a hundred fucking years old?" The words were on the very tip of his tongue ready to roll off. He'd had to be polite for a short eternity with Edith Bennett, and was more than ready to let loose. But he held the words at bay.

Instead, he flashed his badge, saw that the young man's gold-colored nameplate read *Jason Howland,* and said, "Howland, I have a few really quick questions."

Howland recoiled. His eyes widened. "What do you want?"

Sully didn't need fifteen years on the force to recognize the reaction of a guy uncomfortable around cops. Probably because he was guilty of something. Sully guessed steroids. Selling and using. But he didn't have time right now for misdemeanor crimes.

"Frank Bennett," Sully said.

"What about him?"

"What do you know about him?"

Howland's bravado rebounded. "Listen, we're closed.

Come back tomorrow." He took in a deep breath to let his chest swell, and clenched the fist of the arm holding his jacket so his bicep tightened.

Sully figured if he were eighty-five and anyone other than Frank Bennett, he just might shit his pants at the sight of the steroid junkie flexing his muscles. But Sully wasn't eighty-fucking-five and he wasn't about to take any shit from this pissant.

"No I can't come back tomorrow," he snapped. "Frank Bennett is out there somewhere and wind chills are dropping to below zero. If I don't find him, he'll be a fucking icicle tomorrow. I'll come back here and shove that icicle up your fucking ass."

Howland held both hands out. "Chill, man."

"Don't tell me to *chill, man*. Tell me about Bennett and I'll leave you the fuck alone. But there's an eighty-five-year-old man out there who may be freezing to death while you dick around."

"Okay, okay," Howland said. "I'm not sure what there is to say. Frank Bennet is a legend, man. Marathons. Triathlons. A fucking stud. He's lost it upstairs now. His brain, I mean. He'll tell you the same story or the same joke fifteen times in an hour and thinks it's a new one each time. Doesn't recognize anyone. Even the old timers. But a fucking stud. He can still bring it."

"What happened a month or so ago?"

"What?"

"He changed about a month ago."

"You mean the wall?"

Sully blinked. The words "what wall?" were on his tongue and almost slipped out his big mouth. But he swallowed them. Instead, he nodded. "Yeah, the wall. Tell me about it."

"Bennett came in one day all of a sudden excited about climbing. He wanted us to order one of those rock climbing walls, you know? For the gym. You strap into a safety harness in case you fall, and then try to use fake rocks jutting out of the wall as footholds and handholds as you try to climb to the top." Howland shrugged. "He wanted us to order one for the gym so he could become an expert rock climber. I guess he'd done everything else. He wanted to climb."

Sully tried to process the new obsession. "What did you tell him?"

"At first, I was honest. I told him the walls of the gym weren't high enough. But he wouldn't listen. He kept looking on his index card—he couldn't remember shit, so he'd write it down on an index card—and said we needed a rock wall. He wouldn't let up. Just kept saying it over and over. So to shut him up, I told him I'd talk to management."

"Then what happened?"

"We had the exact same conversation the next day. And the day after that. He couldn't remember what I'd told him the day before, so we just went in circles." Howland shrugged. "In one ear, out the other. Until he started writing down on the damned index card what I said. He'd come back the next day and expect progress."

"What did you do?"

Howland smirked. "When he was working out, I'd steal the index card. Set the old fuck back to square one."

Howland began to laugh. "Pretty smart if I may say so myself."

Sully's permanent BOLO for assholes had just found another direct hit. If he were different kind of cop, he'd silence Howland's laughter the hard way, and wipe the smirk off his face and make sure it stayed off. But that was a line Sully didn't cross. He let his bark be worse than his bite.

But it was time for a seriously kick-ass bark.

"Frank Bennett is a greater man than you can ever hope to be," Sully said. "Mock him again, and I'll put you in a fucking hospital."

9:20 p.m.

Edith Bennett looked surprised to see Sully again.

"Most nights I'd be in bed by now," she said from behind the front door. "Did you forget something?"

"No, but I'm hoping you can remember something for me."

"Come in," she said, opening the door wide for him.

Sully shook his head. "This will be quick." He could have added that for all he knew, every minute counted and could be the difference between her husband's life and death. It was cold out there and getting colder. But there was no need to rub her nose in it. She was already a bundle of nerves. "I asked you before if there was anything different about this last month that could have explained your husband's demeanor."

"Yes, and I—"

"What about rock climbing?"

"Rock climbing?" Edith Bennett asked, frowning.

"Rock climbing, mountain climbing. Anything like that."

Her eyes widened. "Mount Everest!"

"Excuse me?"

"He became obsessed with Mount Everest. If he used a computer—he doesn't, but if he did—I'm sure he would have been, what's the word, googling it? Frank saw this one documentary on the TV about climbing Mount Everest, and next thing you know, he was watching an entire series about Everest. Then year two and three of the series. That's all he wanted to watch. Over and over."

Sully had seen a few of them himself. They could become addictive.

"I didn't think it was that big of a deal," Edith said. "We have two TVs so I'd watch something else." Her eyes fell. "I think he watched the same shows over and over. You know, thinking he was watching them for the first time." She smiled weakly. "I didn't think to mention it to you. It didn't seem important. It didn't even occur to me. It's not like he's flown to Nepal or Tibet."

Sully forced a smile to his face. If he had a dollar for every time a witness filtered out useful, sometimes even critical, information based on what *they* thought was important, he'd be on a sunbaked Caribbean beach sipping drinks with tiny umbrellas in them.

Let me *decide what's important*, he wanted to scream. But he couldn't bite Edith Bennett's head off. She'd done the best she could. She was dealing with some seriously tough shit.

"Is it important?" she asked.

———

9:45 p.m.

Sully's fingers were freezing and his lungs exploding. He was too old for this shit. He'd parked the Crown Vic back in the parking lot, having updated Dez on the drive to Lynn Woods, then taken off on a dead run up the path, buttoning his long, black coat with his free hand even as it flapped in the wind. The bright beam from his super-heavy-duty flashlight bounced as it pierced the darkness, but the thing felt like it weighed a hundred fucking pounds.

Stone Tower was only half a mile or so from the parking lot, but it was uphill. And to be honest, Sully had become the anti-Frank Bennett, curling nothing heavier than a brewski, and now he was paying for it. Sully smelled his own sweat, and it would not be bottled anytime soon by Christian Dior or Yves Saint Fucking Laurent. A raw, sour taste filled Sully's mouth.

Frank Bennett was an Ironman; Sully was Marshmallowman.

Somewhere in the distance, an owl hooted. Off to the right, some animal—and not a little one—crashed through the brush. Sully's ragged breathing echoed in the darkness.

He broke into the clearing from which Stone Tower came into view. Five stories tall and thirty feet in diameter, Stone

Tower had been constructed out of stone and mortar almost a century ago as a fire observatory. It rose higher than any other point in Lynn, so Sully was gambling—knowing it was a long-shot—that if Frank Bennett's deteriorating mind wanted to tackle climbing Mount Everest, it might consider Stone Tower the closest thing available, especially since he'd have seen it often in past years during his trail runs through the park.

Sully pointed the flashlight at the octagonal tower, with its arched windows on each floor, each of them closed off by iron gratings. In the foreground, outdoor stairs rose from the ground base to the second floor, then stopped.

He scanned slowly for Frank Bennett. Up and down one side. Up and down another. Up and down all four visible sides.

Bennett was nowhere to be seen.

Sully's shoulders slumped. He felt like a fool. He couldn't believe he'd called the park ranger at home, waking up the poor man who typically arrived at work not long after sunrise because the park was open from six a.m. to sunset. Sully had tried to convince him to crawl out of bed and arrive with keys to unlock the tower so Sully could have access to the interior spiral staircase.

All because...

... there was a one in a thousand chance that an eighty-five-year-old man with dementia might be...

Sully had thought it sounded more and more foolish with every word out of his mouth. He hadn't blamed the park ranger at all when he angrily hung up.

What the hell had he been thinking, Sully wondered, as he got to within a hundred feet of the tower, the stones and gravel crunching beneath his feet. He'd added two plus two and gotten fifteen fucking billion.

If the park ranger contacted the Lieutenant in the morning—correction, *when* the park ranger contacted the Lieutenant in the morning—Sully's ass would be grass. He'd be the laughingstock of the station. Sully could hear the wise-ass remarks now.

Stone Tower. Mount Everest. You can hardly tell them apart! They're almost identical!

Oh, they'd be laughing all right. Sully felt his ears burn even as they stung in the cold. His enemies—and they were plenty—would have a field day.

And the mayor would rake him over the fucking coals. You call yourself a detective? *A detective?* You're nothing but—

Sully stopped. His eyes widened. He was within fifty feet of the tower now, and damned if it didn't look like there was a thick rope hanging down from the rooftop to the second-floor, outside stairwell. He hadn't seen it in the darkness from further away because its dark brown color too closely matched the tower's stones and mortar.

He sprinted forward.

There it was!

Sully moved to the stone stairwell, which only went from the ground up to the second floor, and pointed the flashlight's powerful beam on the thick rope, tethered to the metal railings embedded in the stone-and-mortar on both sides of the stairwell. Ten feet higher, the rope looped into and around the iron gratings sunk into the nearest second-floor windows.

For a moment, Sully stood there, poleaxed, unable to

move or make sense of it all. He looked to the roof, where the rope held taunt.

And then he figured it out.

He dashed around to the back side of the tower and—

There he was! Frank Bennett! High above, at the peak of the top floor, fifty or sixty feet up. One leg over the edge of rooftop. Bennett was straining to pull himself up and over the edge onto the rooftop.

Eyes wide, Sully stared in panic, unable to breathe. What was the old man doing?

But of course, Sully knew exactly what the old man was doing. Frank Bennett was, at least in his mind, summiting Mount Everest.

Sully wanted to yell out a warning, but he couldn't. Didn't dare. Couldn't take a chance of startling the man. Probably make him fall to his death.

So Sully watched in abject terror until, straining mightily—

Frank Bennett pulled himself onto the roof of Stone Tower, and rolled away from the edge.

"I did it!" he called out, standing, raising his arms in triumph, his voice hoarse. He wore a black woolen hat and thick gloves.

Only then did Sully see the rope was also looped and knotted about Bennett's chest and thick winter jacket in something that looked like a version of a bowline knot.

"I did it!" Bennett called out again, pumping his fists, his voice even more hoarse. Sully wondered how many times Bennett had repeated that summiting move then called out his joy, each time turning his throat ever more raw.

What do I do now? Sully wondered. If only the park ranger were actually here with the damned keys. They could get inside and race up the inside spiral staircase that went to the top floor. But did the top floor have an opening to the roof? Sully couldn't recall. It had to, but that hardly mattered, did it? The ranger was still in bed, either having fallen back asleep or was still cursing Sully for waking him up.

Sully pulled out his phone and texted Dez. *Found Bennett. On top of Stone Tower. Need help to get him down. Don't know how.*

Operating on instinct, Sully hollered out to Bennett, "You made it! Congratulations!"

Bennett cupped his gloved hands around his eyes and peered down. He pumped his fist. "I did it! I did it!" He looked off into the distant darkness, perhaps seeing images in his head of surrounding snow-capped Himalayan peaks. "Look at the view!"

"You're on the top of the world!" Sully cried out.

"Yes! Top of the world!" Bennett yelled, his voice getting even more ragged. "Oldest man to do it!"

Sully was about to call out that he was coming up, too. Join Bennett on top of the world. Even though the very thought of getting to the fifth floor and then... *lifting his leg over the edge...* was almost enough to send Sully into cardiac arrest.

But he hadn't become a cop to maximize his life expectancy stats. Sometimes, you gotta do what you gotta do. And he needed to keep Bennett on top of that roof because the next trip down that rope could be his last.

Except that Bennett had the rope tied about his chest in

that modified bowline. Or at least that's how it appeared. If Sully tried climbing up the rope, he'd almost certainly yank Bennett right off the top of the roof. And if the knot didn't hold, or was the wrong type of knot and crushed Bennett's lungs...

Dez supplied the answer. *Ranger and me on way, but 15+ mins out. Keep Bennett talking. Get photos of him on top. Always photos atop Everest.*

Sully checked with the flashlight that Bennett wasn't too close to the edge of the roof, then called out, "Oldest man on top of Everest! Smile for the camera!"

At first, Bennett looked confused. Then he saw Sully with the flashlight in one hand and smartphone in the other. Bennett smiled and pumped his fist. Sully clicked one shot after another. Bennett flashed the number one sign.

"That's great!" Sully yelled. "Oldest man on Everest! How does it feel?"

"Let me see!" Bennett yelled back joyfully.

To Sully's shock and horror, Bennett turned, slipped over the rooftop edge, and began rappelling down the tower wall.

As if he'd done it a hundred times. Which perhaps he had.

Sully's heart lodged in his throat until the old man's feet touched the ground. Bennett slipped out of the bowline and rushed over.

"Let me see! Let me see!" Bennett asked, like a kid about to open a birthday present.

Sully wanted to hug the man, but angled the flashlight so his phone was visible, and flipped through the photos.

"Top of world, Bennett!" Sully cried. "Top of the world!"

Frank Bennett smiled broadly, then suddenly grew serious. "Ready to summit!" he cried. "Have to get to the Hillary Step before the other climbers!"

He hoisted himself back up, feet against the building, not thinking this time to secure a climbing knot about his chest.

Sully wrapped his arms around him. "No!"

Bennett tried unsuccessfully to wriggle free, then looked at Sully, betrayed. "I must go now. It gets crowded at the Hillary Step. I must leave camp now."

Sully held the smaller man tight. "You've already reached the summit, Mr. Bennett. We must descend the rest of the way to Base Camp. It's not safe to stay this high up on the mountain. You need more oxygen."

"I've already reached the summit?"

"Yes, you have! Let me show you the pictures on the way down to Base Camp. Oldest man to summit Everest!

Bennett smiled broadly. "Oldest man to summit Everest!"

Sully guided Bennett toward the path to the parking lot below, slinging an arm around the man's thin shoulders. "A hero's reception awaits you!"

Frank Bennett beamed. "Oldest man to summit Everest!"

ONLY ONE REMAINS

INTRODUCTION TO "ONLY ONE REMAINS"

One of the most common afflictions of aging is memory loss, ranging from mere aggravation at forgotten names and words to the dementia-fueled horrors of those who can no longer recognize family members.

I counted myself so very fortunate that my mom never failed to recognize me. That was such a blessing. Once, near the very end, she didn't use my name, but that was for an absolutely wonderful reason that filled my heart with joy.

I had created a long-standing ritual of bringing seven chocolates to our dinner every week, one for her that night (most often supplemented by another one we would pretend had been intended for me) and the others for each night until I returned.

Weeks before her passing, she lay in a hospital bed as I entered the room. This time, she didn't refer to me by name. Instead, Mom looked at me, smiled, and said, "Chocolates?"

What a wonderful gift.

Another facet of aging, however, isn't the memories lost

but rather the persistence of other memories. That persistence might be of sweet memories that remain a blessing, or sadly, the persistence of horrors that won't go away. Such was the case with my mother's infrequent but haunting recollections of an abusive childhood that came back vividly and viciously. If only those could have been banished forever.

Some memories, however, no matter how haunting, horrific, and painful, must never be forgotten.

ONLY ONE REMAINS

Jacob leans heavily on the iron railing as he eases his thin, frail frame down the subway stairs. He always leads with his good leg, his right leg, then slides the left to flop down beside the right. Step down with the right, flop the left. Step down with the right, flop the left. In truth, there's not much good remaining in the right leg. Both knees pop with almost every feeble step, both keep him up at night with stabbing pain. But the right one is the lesser of two evils.

He wonders if it will give out and he'll tumble like a tattered old rag doll down the remaining dozen or so stairs. Then his tired husk of skin and bones will be shattered into bits and pieces, its sad life leaking away before he even begins this annual pilgrimage.

Down below and off to the left, a train comes screeching into the station. A gust of warm, fetid air blows up into his face, fogging his glasses, and sends his few remaining wisps of white hair whipping about. A stream of people rush past him down the stairs, anxious to catch the train before it leaves. A stocky young man even bumps Jacob's shoulder, almost sending Jacob down those harsh steps to an ignominious demise, but grabs him firmly to steady him, then shakes his head and flees.

Over his shoulder, the young man, who is wearing a navy blue Boston Red Sox cap, shouts, "Sorry, old man, I ain't got all day." Then he is down the last step and racing around the corner.

Jacob nods. Each time he makes this pilgrimage into the bowels of the T, Boston's subway system, he wonders if he'll be granted the entire day.

Whether he deserves it or not.

JACOB WAITS until a suitable train arrives. Since it's five o'clock on a weekday evening—the mass transit equivalent of rush hour—it doesn't take long. One screeches to a halt, and only a good-looking young Black couple step off. This middle car is packed full, every last seat taken and every square inch of floor space filled with wall-to-wall passengers, all of them sardines in a can, grasping onto grimy silver poles, overhanging dirty beige straps, or apparently just trusting their balance.

This is what Jacob needs.

He climbs unsteadily on, even as three other passengers try to squeeze past him and seize what is surely only room for two, the space released by the departed couple. But Jacob holds his ground even as elbows dig into his bony sides and others about him mutter complaints.

This is his train and he will not be denied.

The comments grow even louder and more rude as Jacob shoulders his way toward the middle of the train, wedging himself into spaces less than half his size, careening like a pinball off one body after another with an apology of, "Excuse me, excuse me."

The train starts with a lurch, but Jacob keeps moving toward the middle. Younger men and women—everyone, it seems, is younger than he is—get up from their seats and offer them to him, but he shakes them off.

He has not come here to sit.

A pretty, young woman sees him decline an offer and says with narrowed eyes, "You cop a feel, old man, and it'll be the last thing you ever do."

Jacob nods and detours around her. He collides his way to his desired destination. The middle of the car. Surrounded tightly on all sides. Wedged upright, unable to move. Elbows digging into his ribs on both sides and into his back as well. If he suffers a fatal heart attack, his lifeless body will remain propped up by those around him, unable to collapse to the floor until other passengers disembark.

Sweat streams down his wrinkled face. His arms are pinned to his sides so he can't dry his cheeks, nor can he push his glasses back up to the bridge of his nose. He licks the salty sweat from his lips. The smells of body odor—perhaps his own but more likely the accumulation of what must be almost a hundred passengers in this car—fill the air along with assorted perfumes, colognes, and stale food smells of garlic and onions.

Behind him, unseen, a male voice bellows long and loud, "*Mooooooooo!*"

Others laugh. Yes, this is like a cattle car. Just like a cattle car.

Which is why he is here.

Jacob closes his eyes. His mind goes back the decades to when he was but twelve years old.

THE STENCH of human waste and urine filled the boxcar. Jacob gasped for air. But there was none. He couldn't move. Could only stand there in the overpowering heat and darkness, bodies wedged up against him, one of them Father's bony chest into which Jacob's face was buried. Seven or eight bodies encircled every inch of him, pinning his arms to his sides.

Little two-year-old Abraham, his brother, had been stacked onto Jacob's right shoulder. The German guards at Umschlagplatz had crammed more and more of them in— men, women, and children of all ages—tighter and tighter, until they could squeeze no more in. So Abraham had been tossed on top of Jacob, like a lifeless sack of grain.

At first, Abraham had giggled, as if this were a game. It was not a game.

The boxcar felt like an oven. Baking hot, almost scalding. Without air. Salty sweat stung Jacob's eyes, his head turned away from Father's rough-textured shirt so he could breathe.

The steam locomotive bellowed its chuff-chuff sound as the train accelerated, clicking rhythmically along the tracks. There were no windows, and they'd been locked inside. When they were being loaded in, Jacob had spotted where apparently there had once been a small, square opening high atop the far wall, but rough wooden planks had been hammered over it, enclosing the car as tight as a drum. Tight and airless.

Like a tomb.

Atop Jacob's cramping shoulders, little Abraham cried and gasped for breath. He was not alone. Cries, screams, and panicked gasps echoed inside the wooden walls. Jacob was sure he could hear his sister Rachel, three years older than he was, nearby off to the right with Mother, sobbing.

"I can't breathe," Abraham cried in a panic-filled voice. Choking and gasping, he said again, "I can't breathe!"

"Hush, my son," Mother cooed, nearby but so very far away.

Abraham cried on, his body shaking uncontrollably atop Jacob's shoulders.

"Shhh!" Father said soothingly.

Jacob fought back his own panic. Felt his legs growing weaker and weaker, unable to stand anymore, especially with Abraham's weight atop his shoulders. But the bodies surrounding Jacob held him firmly upright.

He couldn't breathe.

No air! So hot!

No air!

And then sometime later, Jacob knew not when because his head was swimming and his body weak, Abraham's cries became soft whimpers.

And then the whimpers fell silent.

Abraham's little body went slack.

"No!" Father cried. His chest sagged. "No!"

Mother began to weep.

In death, Abraham's body lost all control. The foul smell

of human waste grew even more overpowering. Near and foul. Warm urine poured down Jacob's back.

Jacob shuddered in revulsion and horror. His entire body shook uncontrollably.

Though he was only twelve years old, Jacob knew this boxcar was now a tomb.

WHEN RACHEL'S gasping sobs fell silent, Jacob feared the worst. Surely, it could not be true. First Abraham and now Rachel? The mere thought was like a razor-sharp dagger stabbed into his heart.

Rachel. So good. So true. So wise.

Mother's shriek confirmed Jacob's agonized fear.

His sister was dead.

"No!" Father cried softly, his bony chest wheezing now with every breath. His body shook in anguish. "No!"

Mother wept.

The train clicked rhythmically along the tracks, as if nothing had happened. The steam locomotive bellowed its heartless, uncaring chuff-chuff, chuff-chuff.

And then after a time, Mother fell silent. As had so many other voices in the car.

The train continued its relentless passage. Click-click, click-click, click-click.

"Mother!" Jacob cried out breathlessly, though it seemed no air came back in to fill his lungs. Only the deathly heat and the stench. "Mother!"

She did not answer.

Father's shaking body offered the answer to Jacob's

unspoken question. Mother would hold him no more. She would hold Rachel no more. She would hold little Abraham no more.

Mother was no more.

This trip, for which Father had been forced by the SS to purchase one-way tickets for all but little Abraham, would end in the death of them all.

There was no avoiding it.

The boxcar fell silent as the tomb it had become, a silence broken only by the wheezing of lungs and the cries and prayers of a few.

Outside, the train continued on its unfeeling tracks. Click-click, click-click, click-click.

"Jacob, my son!" Father wheezed in the softest of whispers. "My son!"

He gave a final shudder, and then he, too, fell silent.

Leaving only Jacob.

JACOB PULLS BACK from the memory, and that of all the dead bodies hauled out of the train when they reached Auschwitz. Abraham, Rachel, Mother, and Father. All of the others.

All stacked in a heap like a pile of trash, ready to be collected.

Jacob realizes he is wheezing now, here in this Boston subway car, wheezing like Father had those eight decades ago.

A sound Jacob will never forget.

The subway car, no longer packed like a sardine can

after unloading passengers at the last few stops, screeches into the final stop on the route.

The end of the line.

And so Jacob totters off the car, and lurches his way amidst the litter scattered on the grime-covered concrete platform, the humid smell of stale sweat in his nostrils. He heads to the opposite side so he can return to where he began this pilgrimage, his tribute to his family complete.

Each year, he asks himself why he does this. Why risk incapacitating injury from a fall? Why risk a mugging? Why rip his heart out over and over, year after year?

Yes, he made himself a promise all those years ago when he was the only member of his family to emerge from that train still alive—the only one who wasn't tossed onto that heap of dead bodies—and then avoided the gas chambers by dint of his strength at forced labor even as his body wasted away until he looked skeletal by the time the camp was liberated.

It was a promise to never forget. Never forget Abraham, Rachel, Mother, Father, and all the others in that Boxcar of Death, and all the others like it that arrived there in Auschwitz and the other camps, and sent almost all their occupants to the gas chambers.

It's a promise he has kept. He will never forget. But must he remember in this way even as his body becomes more and more frail?

Jacob doesn't know for sure, but he has always sensed in the deepest recesses of his soul that to truly remember their murders by the Nazis in that Boxcar of Death, he must each year on the anniversary of that day, board a train and once again feel the terror of being enclosed by bodies on all sides and all the horrors that came to mean.

He will never understand why the others were taken and he was not.

Why little Abraham, and not him? Why Rachel, so kind and sweet, and not him? Why Mother and Father, and not him?

He does not deserve to be here. They did not deserve to die on that train.

He wonders if perhaps it is enough that his soul was slaughtered along with their bodies on that day. For it most certainly was. But he doubts it.

There are no answers.

He knows only that he will never forget.

WALK AWAY EVEN

INTRODUCTION TO "WALK AWAY EVEN"

This story came out of an assignment to write a "Last Job" mystery/crime story. The criminal might or might not be coming out of retirement, might or might not be dying, but this most certainly would be his last job. After this, he would be done forever.

Given my concerns with aging, the direction for "Walk Away Even" was obvious before I even sat down to type the first word. I won't say the story wrote itself. As usual, I took a few million wrong turns as I learned about my characters and how this last job would unfold.

But as I wrote, I fell in love with Willie O'Rourke. For a writer, that's pure gold. I rooted like hell that he would, in the end, walk away even.

WALK AWAY EVEN

Willie O'Rourke looked through his apartment's peephole. Didn't recognize the guy. But that didn't mean anything. He didn't recognize anybody these days. Some mornings, he got out of bed, took fifteen minutes to pee, then looked in the mirror and wondered who the hell that ugly old geezer was.

Not this morning, though. This morning he was sharp, or at least as sharp as he ever got. Sharp enough to recognize himself in the mirror.

Time for the Hallelujah Chorus and a party.

Willie squinted again through the peephole. The man standing in the hallway outside his apartment here in Golden Acres might look familiar after all. An old fart just like him, though not quite as old.

Not eighty-nine, teetering on the awful precipice of the big nine-oh-crap. Willie remembered the days—well, he didn't *really* remember them, but he had a vague sense of being alive back then—when he'd feared the big four-oh. And then the big five-oh.

Child's play! That's what those had been. You want scary, you thirty-nine-year-old whiner? Try looking out over the cliff's edge and look way down to the rock bottom of the big nine-oh-crap. It's so far down, you can barely see a thing. Is that even a rocky floor or is it just black nothingness?

Stare down at it too long and you get dizzy. Get dizzy and you fall right off the cliff.

And that's the name of that tune.

Willie furrowed his brow.

What tune? The name of what tune?

Confused, he looked off to the right as if somehow the answer—what tune?—might be there. Saw all the framed pictures on the wall. Was pretty sure they were all his children, grandchildren, and great-grandchildren, though he doubted he could recall most of their names. Lots of pictures of Betty, his deceased wife. A sweetheart. God, how he missed her. Bright red hair and a big smile. He could never forget her.

He hoped he'd never forget her.

Willie turned to walk back into the living room. What was he even doing here at the door? He couldn't remember.

He had to pee.

The doorbell chimed. Willie vaguely recalled it sounding just a few minutes ago. Or had that been hours? Or days?

Who the hell knew anymore? Sure as Sherlock not him.

He leaned close to the peephole and squinted. A guy with a full head of white hair just like himself. This wasn't a mirror, was it? Willie leaned back to look at the door to be sure and almost fell over backwards.

Staggering, he righted himself. Then leaned back in again. Looked through the peephole. No, not a mirror. This guy was younger than he was. A younger dinosaur. Maybe seventy to his own big nine-oh-crap. Chubby, at least fifty pounds overweight. Definitely not a mirror. Willie was nothing but skin and bones. He looked down at himself to double-check. Yeah, nothing but skin and bones and liver spots on his wrinkled, skinny hands. The guy out in the hallway was wearing a black suit and red tie.

A suit and tie? To visit him? Probably a salesman.

Willie looked down and saw he was still dressed in his bathrobe and slippers. It was what? He looked at his watch. Ten o'clock. AM or PM? AM. Had to be. Willie was almost positive. And there'd been no reason to get dressed.

Had there? Or was this guy here for an appointment that he'd forgotten? He should check his appointment book.

Willie turned to totter back to the kitchen table where he kept his appointment book. God knows why he bothered. Just one empty page after another staring back at him. Telling him there was nothing for him to do. Get out of bed, walk from the bedroom to here in the living room and to the kitchen. Then go back. Stop at the bathroom each time on the way to pee.

Could life get any more exciting?

At least he didn't need anything in that damned blank appointment book to remind him to pee. No sir. But perhaps he should fill the appointment book with peeing reminders. Not that he needed them. But fill the blank pages.

It was a good idea. The best he'd had in years. He'd better write it down before he forgot it.

"Put pee reminders in the book," Willie said aloud so he wouldn't forget, lurching toward the kitchen. "Put pee reminders in the book."

The doorbell chimed.

Damn, he sure was getting a lot of visitors today. Or was this the first?

Willie turned toward the door, telling himself not to forget what he'd been trying to remember, what he'd been repeating so he wouldn't forget. He needed to pee in the book.

He frowned. That didn't make sense even to him. Pee in what book? And why would he want to pee in a book? Wouldn't that ruin it?

Nothing made sense anymore.

Willie looked into the peephole, feeling an odd sense of *déjà vu*. There was a guy in a suit in the hallway. Maybe he looked familiar, maybe not. It was hard to tell, looking through the peephole glass. It distorted the view.

Though wasn't everything distorted these days? Hadn't it been great way back in the days of perfect clarity? Willie supposed it had, but damned if he could remember.

The doorbell chimed again.

"Willie, it's Deke," boomed a voice through the door. "Open up, you old bastard!"

The suited figure in the hallway grinned broadly and flipped Willie the bird.

"Willie, you're number one," the voice said.

Deke!

Then the grinning figure—*Deke!*—raised the back of

his other hand and extended his other middle finger. He waved them both at Willie.

"No, Willie, you ain't number one," the voice said. "You're number eleven."

Deke!

The notches lined up magically on the interlocking wheels.

Deke! Of course! Well, why hadn't he said so?

Willie joyfully opened the door, a broad grin on his face. "Deke, how have you been, you old bastard?"

Deke recoiled, then spread his arms open wide and they hugged.

"Who you calling old?" Deke said, laughing and slapping Willie's shoulder. "Look at you!"

Willie looked at himself and shrugged. He cocked his head. Had there been a question there?

"You look like crap," Deke said with a laugh, though it seemed that a trace of uneasiness ran through his laughter. "When's the last time you shaved? And when's the last time you showered? You're a little... um... ripe."

Willie felt his face grow hot. He wasn't exactly sure when he had last shaved or showered. There'd hardly been a point. Why bother?

So now here he was in front of Deke—*Deke!*—looking and smelling like a useless old man who couldn't take care of himself.

And maybe that's just what he was. A useless old man who couldn't take care of himself.

Willie fumbled on what to say.

"I've been busy," he said, knowing it sounded lame. "If I'd known you were coming, I'd have—"

"Forget it!" Deke said, waving the explanation aside, but still looking wary. He clapped Willie on the shoulder. "I should have called."

"No, no!" Willie cried. "It's great to see you. I'm sorry I look so... so... as you said so eloquently, sorry I look like crap."

"Don't worry about it!" Deke laughed. "You were ugly as sin even in the best of times."

Willie almost hugged Deke again, but then remembered —*actually remembered something!*—that he apparently stank to high heavens so he froze, only halfway toward an embrace.

"Can we talk inside?" Deke asked.

DEKE SIPPED his coffee and looked across the kitchen table at his old friend. Deke had tried to make a joke of it, but Willie looked horrible. Shockingly bad. There was no hiding it. White hair sticking up every which way like in the "Crazy Einstein" photo. Gaunt, unshaven face. An overall haggard appearance. The apartment stifling hot despite the seasonable May weather outside. And the smell!

Deke put the coffee cup to his lips and held it there, as steady as his hands could manage, breathing it in deeply through his nostrils to try cancel out the odor of piss and decay in the apartment.

And in Willie himself.

The view out the window to the left was pleasant enough—two oak trees and a grassy lawn separating two other wings of the brick, four-story, Golden Acres apartments—but the sink to the right and the stove behind Willie were both piled high with dirty dishes. Somewhere in one of those stacks reeked a pool of sour, rancid milk. Unless somehow, even worse, that stench was leaking out of the humming refrigerator to the right.

Shocking.

There was no other word for it. Although, in truth, there was another, even more accurate, word for it.

Heartbreaking.

Willie had once been the best in the business. Now, you clearly couldn't entrust him to simply take out the garbage.

Heartbreaking.

"It's been a long time," Willie said, grinning broadly.

It was the third time he'd made the same comment in the last two minutes.

"Feels like forever," Deke said, speaking truthfully.

If even a glimmer of the Willie of old could be found, Deke was having a tough time spotting it.

"You're looking great," Willie said, also for the third time in the last two minutes.

It felt like a science fiction movie where aliens had taken over Willie's body and he was speaking in a recorded loop.

"Can I get you more coffee?" Willie asked, another line in the recorded loop. "If you're hungry, I can see if there's something in the fridge."

"No, no, no," Deke said, not wanting to think of the overpowering stench that might gush out of the refrigerator and linger in his nostrils for days. His mind involuntarily went back to a ripe, dead body back in the day.

Deke shuddered. His stomach heaved.

"You cold?" Willie asked, apparently noticing the shudder. "I can turn the heat up."

"Oh, no," Deke said. The apartment was already stifling hot. "I'm fine."

Deke had been trying to set up as quick and diplomatic of an exit as possible. Willie could be of no use. He was just too far gone. *Way* too far gone. If Stella had had any idea, she'd have never sent him here on this fool's errand.

Except...

Willie *had* noticed Deke's shudder, prompting the question of if he was cold. There was *something* still left there. Willie was only a shell of his former self—a horrifyingly near-empty shell—but some fragment remained. A microscopic fragment perhaps, but Deke's cold assessment moments earlier of "lights out, no one's home" wasn't totally accurate.

There was still *some* light flickering there.

"It's been a long time," Willie said yet again. "It's great to see you!"

So much for that flickering light reassessment, Deke thought ruefully. This had been a waste of time. Nothing but a sad, social visit. The saddest gut-punch of a visit he could remember.

"You're looking great," Willie said, again.

Deke grinned weakly.

"Can I get you more coffee?" Willie asked, and slurped noisily on his own. "Heat yours up a bit?"

Only then did Deke notice how steady Willie's hand remained as he slurped away like a preschooler guzzling his chocolate milk.

Almost all the lights were out. *Almost* no one was home.

But Willie's hands were still solid as a rock. Not even a hint of a tremor. And his hearing was just fine.

Deke wanted to kick himself. He'd let Willie's appalling physical appearance and the two-minute-time-loop aspect to most of his conversation blind him, Deke, from what really mattered.

Hands and ears.

Willie had never been the brains of the team. Thank God. He'd been their master safecracker. The best in the business.

So what if only one light still flickered in Willie's chandelier of the mind? As long as that lone bulb didn't wink out and his hands remained steady, this might just work.

Besides, Deke thought, who was he kidding? He and Stella were stuck. No other safecracker would take the job. Just not worth their while. If Willie couldn't do it, there was no job. Perhaps Willie's most forceful endorsement.

"It's been a long time," Willie said, smiling. "Great to see you again!"

Tune out the loop, Deke told himself. Eyes on the prize. He leaned forward.

"Willie, do you think you can still crack a safe?" Deke asked. Best to get right to the point. Any subtlety would be lost on Willie.

Willie blinked in obvious surprise.

"Crack a safe? Sure." Elbow on the table, he rubbed his right thumb against his two forefingers, usually a reference to money, and perhaps that was what he was doing, his depleted mind now making an accustomed connection between cracking a safe and a payday. But it seemed to Deke that this was more of a warming up of Willie's fingers, like licking one's lips before a tasty meal. Willie beamed. "It's like riding a bicycle. You never forget how to fall off."

Deke winced inwardly at the butchered cliché but tried to conceal his unease. Eyes on the prize.

"There's a job," Deke said.

Willie's eyes lit up like exploding suns. "*A job? Really? For me?*"

"It won't pay much. I'll have to pay you out of my own pocket, and things are a little tight right now. But it's a job."

"Okay," Willie said. He leaned forward, forearms on the table, eyes ablaze, as eager as a teenage boy awaiting the punchline to a dirty joke. "*A job for me? Really?*"

"Do you remember my wife Stella?" Deke asked.

All the joy rushed out of Willie's suddenly ashen face, replaced by a look of disappointment and outright betrayal. Eyes haunted, he looked about to cry. "I'm confused."

"You don't remember Stella?" Deke asked.

"I thought you were talking about a job," Willie said, breathing noisily though his nose. "A job for me."

"I am," Deke said, trying to sound reassuring. "Some bad people stole something important from my wife Stella."

"Stella," Willie said. "Big boobs. Big butt."

Deke laughed. "Yeah, that's her. They stole something from her. I want you to help me steal it back."

"Me?" Willie said, pointing to his chest, eyebrows raised in disbelief.

"Yes," Deke said. "Us. The two of us will steal it back. Together."

"What are we going to steal back?"

"My wife's jewelry," Deke said. "Two days ago, a couple of thieves named the Balducci brothers broke into our house and stole it. A few of the pieces are quite expensive. I just want to get back what's mine. Walk away even."

Willie blinked. "Are they insured?"

"No." Deke sighed. "All the expensive ones are pieces I stole myself over the years, waited till things cooled down each time, then gave to Stella as gifts. So I couldn't insure them, and of course, I can't report the robbery to the cops. The only way to get them back is to steal them back. I'm going to pay you out of my own pocket to do that. Fortunately, I already know where they are. In a safe on the outskirts of town. In Rocco and Butchie Balducci's basement on Chestnut Lane."

"How did you find that out?"

"Just like the old days, I have my sources." Deke shrugged. "Rocco tried to fence the jewelry, but didn't like the offer. He thought he was getting stiffed. That's Rocco. He always thinks he's getting stiffed. So he's playing hardball. But we'll have to move fast. He ain't gonna hold onto them forever."

Willie nodded slowly, but Deke wondered how much his old friend really comprehended.

"One other thing," Deke said. "There's a necklace. It's of very little financial value, only a couple hundred dollars, but it's worth more to Stella than all the other pieces combined. It's of great sentimental value. That's the one piece she insists on getting back. It's... um... it's a custom necklace that holds... well... it holds her mother's cremation ashes. She's very upset that she's lost it."

A troubled look filled Willie's eyes. "I'm confused."

"About what?"

"About everything. I don't understand."

"Someone took Stella's jewelry," Deke said, trying to keep his tone even without sounding like he was talking to a two-year-old. "It's in a safe. You're going to help me get it back."

"Who's Stella?"

Deke felt the air go out of his lungs. "Stella's my wife. Remember? Big boobs. Big butt."

Willie nodded but looked lost.

"Willie, all you have to do is crack open the safe. I'll take care of everything else."

Willie stared off into the distance.

"What's wrong?" Deke asked.

"You've been a good friend to me, Deke," Willie said, looking mournful. "A great friend. So I've got to be honest. I don't know if you can count on me. My brain doesn't work so good anymore."

Really? I hadn't noticed! The sarcasm flooded Deke's mind, but he gently said, "You'll do fine."

"I'm confused almost all the time," Willie said. "I'm trying to hold on but I feel it all slipping away. I don't know if you can trust me anymore." He screwed up his face and looked about to cry. "I don't know if I can trust myself anymore. Sometimes... I'm not sure I'm really still here."

Deke grasped his friend's hand and squeezed hard.

"Don't worry," Deke said. "We'll do this together. A team. Like old times. There's also a woman who's going to distract the Balducci brothers."

"Stella?" Willie asked.

"No," Deke said, closing his eyes and shaking his head. "Forget her. Forget about everything else. You only need to crack the safe. Just that one thing. Can you still crack a safe for me?"

Willie nodded.

———

DEKE SAID it was like the old days, him behind the wheel of his black Cadillac, and Willie riding shotgun, but Willie wasn't so sure. He remembered some of the old days vividly but most of them were just lost in the fog of his memory. He didn't remember riding shotgun. He didn't remember even holding a shotgun. Only pistols and revolvers. And he certainly wasn't holding a shotgun now.

It was all so confusing. And he had to pee.

"Can we go now?" Willie asked. The air in the darkened car felt close and heavy. His long-sleeved, button-down black shirt clung to his skin.

"No!" Deke said. "I'll tell you when it's set."

They were parked diagonally across from the Balducci bothers' house on Chestnut Lane, a remote side street lined with thick growths of pine, oak, and birch trees separating expensive-looking homes spaced far apart. Street lighting up ahead and behind them poked through the darkness but left Deke's parked car in the shadows. There were no other cars on the street. No other cars anywhere except for the driveways of two houses in the distance.

This was five miles from Golden Acres, but for Willie, the five miles might as well be five hundred thousand. He couldn't remember the last time he'd left the confines of his retirement community. He felt like an escaped convict.

But an escaped convict still trapped inside Deke's Cadillac.

Willie itched to get out. He couldn't wait to get his fingers on the dial of a safe again. Couldn't wait to twist its cold dial. Couldn't wait to hear in his ears the magical clicking of the notches once again.

He was *on the job*! His heart pounded. He couldn't wait to get going. Couldn't stop rubbing his thumb and two forefingers together.

And he had to pee.

"What are we waiting for?" he asked.

"I told you we need to wait five more minutes to be sure the agents in the meat have knocked out the Rottweilers."

"What's an agent?" Willie asked.

Deke ignored him. "And we need to wait for me to get a call from Heather, letting me know the Balducci boys are indisposed."

"Who's Heather?"

"The third member of our team," Deke said, sighing. "That's not even her real name. You've never met her before, you're not meeting her tonight, and you'll never meet her in the future."

"Why?"

"It's better that way."

"Does Stella know about Heather?"

"Stop asking questions!"

"Is Heather killing the Balducci brothers?"

Deke's head whipped around to face Willie.

"Of course not!" Deke said. "We're not killers. We're just taking back what is mine. Heather's slipping something into their drinks to put them out of action for a while.

They'll wake up with nothing more than a headache, then come home to an empty safe."

"Does Stella know about Heather?"

"Give it a rest!"

Willie tried to give it a rest. He could tell he was annoying Deke, but everything was so confusing. Of course he had questions. Did Heather have big boobs and a big butt like Stella? Why wouldn't Deke answer whether Stella knew about Heather? What if the agents—whatever agents were, something like secret agents?—didn't knock out the Rottweilers?

So many questions. And eventually, Deke's answers always came down to just "crack the safe and leave the rest to me."

Willie wanted to get going. The safe in that house was practically calling his name. Begging him to come. He was tired of waiting. And he had to pee.

"Can we go now?" Willie asked.

"No!" Deke snapped.

"I've got to pee."

"You're wearing your Depends, right?" Deke said, his voice overflowing with annoyance. Even more overflowing than Willie's bladder.

"Yes, but I don't like—"

"Then use them and shut up! You're driving me crazy!"

Willie felt his face grow warm. He didn't mean to drive Deke crazy. So he did what he was told. Soon his crotch felt as warm as his face.

Deke's phone rang.

"You're sure?" he said into the phone. And then, "Good!"

Deke turned to Willie. "All set. Let's go."

They both grabbed off the backseat a cigar-sized, black flashlight and a black leather doctor's bag. They crossed Chestnut diagonally to the Balduccis' two-story house. An outdoor porch light shone brightly as did a single lamp inside, visible through the curtained, front picture window.

Willie saw a pistol stuffed into the waistband of Deke's dark pants. It had been many years since the last time Willie had held a pistol. He didn't dare hold one now. Only bad things could happen. He hoped Deke wouldn't have to use his.

Willie breathed in deeply of the pine-scented air and hurried to keep up. He tried to calm his pounding heart, but it didn't work, and not just because this was the farthest and fastest he'd walked in a long time.

He was *on the job* again!

Alive again!

His heart hammered even harder, even faster. Willie opened his mouth wide and sucked in a big gulp of air. He hoped he didn't suffer a heart attack before he got his hands on that safe.

They approached a waist-high, square, metal fence surrounding the dark brown house. Deke rattled it.

Nothing.

Deke drew the pistol. Willie thought it might be a Glock, but couldn't remember why. Just somehow knew. Deke reached over the metal gate, jiggled something, and opened it.

Willie licked his lips. The inside of his head throbbed.

Deke scanned the yard, then motioned Willie to follow him to the back. Willie did what he was told. They walked past two black Rottweilers, barely visible in the shadows cast by the street lighting, sleeping on their sides, their tongues hanging out.

On the unlighted backdoor porch, they both turned on the small but powerful cigar-sized flashlights. Holding them in their left hands, they pointed them on the backdoor lock. Deke put his bag down and set to work.

"When we get in, I'll get the alarm and check the rest of the house," Deke said. "Like we've gone through a million times, you go down the stairs. No lights. Only the flashlight. Watch your step. If there's a railing, put the flashlight in your mouth and use the damned railing. You're a dead man if you fall. The safe is off to your left near the water heater. Understand?"

Willie nodded so hard he though his head might fall off.

On the job! Alive! His lungs felt like they might explode.

"Repeat what I said!" Deke said, treating him like a two-year-old.

Willie proved he wasn't a two-year-old, repeating it word for word, pretty sure they'd repeated the words over and over back inside the car. "Down the stairs. Flashlight my mouth. Railing. I'm a dead man. Safe to the left. Water heater."

"Close enough," Deke said, shaking his head. "Keep repeating it so you don't forget. If you do forget, it's written on your instructions."

Willie patted his left pants pocket with the fingers wrapped around the flashlight. The beam of light wobbled wildly, but he felt the outline of two pens and the small memo pad holding blank sheets and the instructions.

"Fall down the stairs," Willie said, repeating as ordered.

"Flashlight the railing in my mouth. Dead man. Safe to the left next to the water heater." He understood completely. "Fall down the stairs. Flashlight my mouth. Railing. Dead man. Safe to the left. Water heater."

Deke swore softly.

"Fall down the stairs," Willie said. "Flashlight the—"

Deke opened the door. He bolted inside.

Willie spotted Deke's beam of light focused momentarily on a closed door to what had to be the basement stairs ten feet straight ahead.

"There!" Deke said softly, and was gone.

Willie tottered to the basement door. Sweat beaded on his forehead. As he put his bag of tools down, his back creaked, but a huge smile covered his face.

On the job!

He opened the basement door and trained the flashlight beam on a dark wooden railing attached to the right wall.

"Fall down the stairs," Willie said, then kept himself from repeating any more reminders by cramming the flashlight into his mouth and biting down on it with his teeth. Like a cigar, he told himself, even though the hard plastic tasted nothing like a cigar. It tasted like sweat and felt uncomfortable as hell, but orders were orders.

Breathing noisily through his nose, he grasped the tool bag with his left hand and reached for the handrail with the other.

With each step down the stairs, he leaned more and more heavily on the handrail. His knees creaked, threatening to buckle beneath him.

Fall down the stairs, he reminded himself. Dead man.

Willie wheezed as he tried unsuccessfully to suck

enough air in through his nose. His nostrils burned. His heart raced even faster.

Would he make it to the bottom of the stairs where he could remove the damned flashlight—not like a cigar at all!—from his mouth? He'd make it for certain, Willie knew that. But would he get there falling and tumbling head over heels the rest of the way, breaking his neck and half the other bones in his body? Or would he make it still standing?

Fall down the stairs, he reminded himself. Dead man.

The beam of light shooting out of his mouth wobbled. He couldn't see the base of the stairs. Salty sweat stung his eyes. His lungs felt ready to explode.

On the job! he reminded himself. *Alive!*

Willie took another creaking, painful step down even as his head swam.

Back with the team! Even though the team now consisted only of him and Deke. And some woman, wasn't it? Was it Stella? Or...

Didn't matter.

Deke had made that clear even to Willie's addled mind. Willie only needed to get down those stairs and crack the safe. Leave the rest to Deke and Stella. Or whoever the woman was.

Fall down the stairs, Willie reminded himself. Dead man.

Finally, what felt like an eternity later, he reached the bottom step. Willie felt no euphoria, only relief. He spat the flashlight into his hand and gasped. He gulped for air. His chest heaved. He barely noticed how drenched with warm saliva the flashlight was in his hands.

Dizzy, Willie wobbled. Sweat poured off his face. He blinked the salty sting out of his eyes.

The stairs had been like climbing Everest. The air sure was thin up here. Almost no oxygen. He could barely breathe.

He almost collapsed back onto the stairs behind him. Wanted to. Wanted it so bad.

Sit there for just for a moment, he told himself. At least until he got his breath. Just a few seconds. What could it hurt? Give him a chance to remember whatever it was he was supposed to do next.

The thought was as seductive as a beautiful woman. Intoxicating. Willie could barely conceive of a reason not to drop back down and relieve his trembling legs.

The safe! flashed into his mind. *You're on the job!*

Suddenly, Willie somehow knew that if he sat down here in this darkness broken only by his flashlight's wobbling light, he would never get up.

The safe! That's what he was here to do! *Crack the safe!* One last time, do what God had put him on this Earth to do.

The cold, metal dial of the safe called to him. The clicking of the notches called to him, whispering sweetly, seductively.

Wiping the sweat away from his eyes with his shirtsleeve, Willie tottered toward the far corner of the dank, musty basement. He pointed his flashlight's thin beam at first one wall and then another, searching for the beloved view of a safe begging him to open its door.

One last time.

He couldn't see it! The thin beam of light shone only

on gray concrete walls. Then a filing cabinet. A battered old desk and chair. More bare concrete walls.

Anything but a safe.

Panic rose within Willie's chest. His breathing, ragged and gasping back at the base of the stairs, had begun to quiet, but now it quickened again.

He couldn't find the safe!

Where was it? A beautiful, gleaming metal safe. Or one rusted and covered with dust or even mold. *Any* safe. The love of his life, even greater than Betty!

And then the beam of light blissfully caught it, reflecting off the metal dial.

Willie gasped for joy. It was next to a white, cylindrical water heater. Had that been something he was supposed to remember?

Didn't matter. He'd found it!

Even as the beam of his flashlight wobbled, Willie lurched toward the safe and its beautiful metal dial, awaiting its embrace.

It took forever to get there.

Willie knelt in front of it, as if ready to worship at its altar. He placed his memo pad on the cold, concrete floor between his knees. On it, he would write notes using the pen clenched between his teeth. He would record positions on the dial he'd have held in his head in years past but tonight would slip through his memory like sand through one's fingers. Tonight, paper would hold what his mind could not.

Willie removed the stethoscope from his bag of tools and placed its earpieces in both his ears. He held the stethoscope's bell against the safe's metal wall.

Sweat poured off his face. His arthritic knees throbbed with pain, the cold surface of the rough concrete floor sending icy daggers up his thighs into his hips and down to his toes. With every slight movement, the skin on his kneecaps rubbed raw.

Willie did not care. He barely noticed the discomfort.

This was bliss.

He bathed the safe's dial in the spotlight of his flashlight's beam. Willie turned the cold knob, feeling a dreamlike peace and a mental clarity he hadn't felt in... in an eternity. All was clear to him now.

The sound of the notches lining up was like a symphony to his ears. He was a maestro conducting an orchestra. Beethoven's ninth, this was! He was Ted Williams hitting a home run in his final at bat. Bill Russell, securing an eleventh NBA championship in his final season.

Willie made love to the dial and it cried out its joy at his touch. He rotated it counterclockwise, heard the two clicks near each other, one fainter than the other, and scribbled the position on the pad of paper. He caressed the dial several revolutions clockwise, then again listened for its orgiastic clicks as he slowly fingered it counterclockwise.

It had been true. Like riding a bicycle or making love to a woman, you never forgot how.

Willie parked the wheel—

A hand lightly touched him on the shoulder. Willie cried out in terror. The pen clattered from his mouth to the concrete floor. The flashlight fell from his grasp. Warmth filled his crotch.

Deke's face appeared over Willie's shoulder, illuminated by his flashlight. Patting Willie's shoulder in reassurance,

Deke moved all the way around to Willie's left. He gave a thumbs up.

Deke!

Willie's terror turned to rage. Molten rage that Deke had interrupted the seduction of the tumblers. *Dammit, Deke!* Willie wanted to strangle him. Rage flooded his mind.

He only resumed breathing, not realized that he had ever stopped, when he saw Deke pick up the pen to take over the scribbling of notes and point his own flashlight on the safe's so very beautiful dial.

The seduction resumed. Willie wanted it never to end.

He felt almost disappointed when the safe door opened.

BACK IN THE Cadillac before they entered the Balduccis' house, Deke had thought he might shoot Willie if the old geezer didn't shut up.

"Can we go now?"

"What are we waiting for?"

"Who is Heather?"

"Does Stella know about Heather?"

Willie had been like a ten-year-old about to start a summer vacation, asking questions before the rear tires had even left the driveway. Are we there yet? Are we there yet? Are we there yet?

Wanted to shoot the guy.

But now, watching the safe door open bathed in the beam his flashlight, Deke wanted to kiss Willie.

The sight was breathtaking. Literally. Deke held a hand to his chest, unable to breathe.

The jewelry! All of it visible inside a canvas sack, from the most expensive piece to the necklace that was special only because it held the cremation ashes.

But not just the jewelry. There were stacks of banded hundred dollar bills. There had to be hundreds of thousands of dollars. There were also packets of a white powdery substance that had to be cocaine. Deke couldn't even guess at the street value. He never touched the stuff, either as a user or a dealer, but even if he offloaded it at only forty or fifty cents on the dollar, he'd make a mint.

He wouldn't just be walking away even. The safe was a gold mine.

He shoved the sack of jewelry into Willie's mostly empty leather bag, then grabbed a packet of bills. Fanned the Benjamins. What a beautiful sight! He shoved the packet into his own leather bag and grabbed another. And another.

"Don't just kneel there," Deke commanded, euphoric exuberance in his voice. "Load up!"

Willie stared back blankly, the stethoscope still attached to his ears. He looked suddenly pale and lifeless in the meager light of the flashlights.

"We aren't taking just the jewelry?" Willie asked.

"Of course not," Deke replied. "If we only take the jewelry, they'll know it was me. If *everything* gets stolen, then it could be anybody. Besides, look at all this cash. And the coke. Not even Mother Teresa could turn down a payday like this."

Willie blinked. "Not just the jewelry?"

A simpleton, Deke thought, and felt a pang of sadness. That's what his old friend had been reduced to. Willie had had it all back in the day and still—thank god!—retained enough of his magic touch to crack this safe. But now Willie was just a used up old man with a feeble chandelier of the mind every bit as dark as this basement. Wearing a Depends soaked in his own piss.

"Not just the jewelry!" Deke snapped, feeling bad at verbally taking the geezer's head off but needing to get him moving. "Hurry up!"

"Even the drugs?" Willie asked.

"Everything!"

Bright light suddenly flooded the basement.

Deke felt his blood run cold. He whirled to look toward the stairs, pulling the Glock from inside his waistband. He pointed it toward the stairs, but only the lower half of the stairs was visible.

No one was in sight.

A gravelly voice boomed from the top of the stairs, out of sight. "You didn't really think Rocco and Butchie would leave all their loot unguarded, did you? They may be stupid, but they ain't that stupid."

WHEN THE SAFE DOOR OPENED, Willie felt all the energy leak out of him. He'd never felt more alive than when he'd been cracking that safe. Adrenaline had coursed through his veins.

But as soon as he'd opened the safe door, it had felt as though an electrical plug had been pulled. One second, he'd been brimming with energy and life. As vital as in the good old days.

The next, nothing.

Now, hearing the booming voice at the top of the stairs, Willie wasn't sure what to think. Was the plug about to get pulled on his entire life? His and Deke's?

"I got a loaded shotgun here and two more of me are on the way," boomed the gravelly voice from atop the stairs, out of sight. "And there ain't no other way out from down there. So you two geezers might as well come up here and take your medicine."

The unmistakable, chilling sound of a shotgun being racked echoed through the basement.

Deke looked like he was about to collapse. Wide, haunted eyes. He'd pulled the Glock out but was looking at it now as if it were little more than water pistol. And compared to a shotgun, it wasn't much more. Deke's gun hand shook.

Willie wasn't feeling much better. Apparently, he wasn't going to make it to the big *nine-oh-crap* after all. He'd been teetering on that precipice, staring at the darkness down below, and now here it came. Racing up at him.

For reasons he didn't understand, just acting on instinct, Willie reached into the jewelry sack inside his leather bag and pulled out what was quite clearly the necklace with the mother-in-law's ashes. A gold chain and circular locket that had to contain the ashes. Willie turned it around. Something was inscribed on the back inside the shape of a heart. He couldn't read the fine lettering, but he guessed it was the mother-in-law's date of birth and death.

His own Betty had been buried, not cremated, but Willie wished he owned something like this necklace—a more masculine version, of course—to remember her by. Something to be wearing when the guy at the head of the stairs pointed that shotgun at him and pulled the trigger.

"This is the one with the ashes?" he asked Deke in a whisper.

Deke looked at Willie like he was just a bug. And maybe that's all he was anymore, Willie thought. Just an annoying mosquito buzzing around just waiting to get slapped.

But Deke nodded.

Willie looped the necklace around his neck. He tucked the locket inside his button-down shirt so it was out of sight. He patted it.

"Toss your guns to the foot of the stairs and I just might let you live," the voice from the top of the stairs said. "Otherwise, I shoot first, ask questions later."

Deke stood there frozen, Glock in his hand, staring at it blankly.

Willie peered into the canvas sack, held it open wide, and pawed at the remaining jewelry. Expensive-looking stuff.

The clarity of mind he'd felt while cracking the safe surged back into him like a jolt of electricity.

Was any of this expensive jewelry *really* worth anything? If he was about to get blow into bits—both him and Deke —did even the most expensive jewelry or the cash or the cocaine really matter?

He patted the ashes in the locket looped around his neck.

"Toss your gun, Deke," Willie said. "He might shoot us anyway, but it's our only chance."

Deke snapped out of his frozen state and whirled on Willie.

"*You're* telling *me* what to do?" Deke whispered, fury in his eyes. "I've had to babysit you all damned night. Now *you're* telling *me* what to do? Go piss in your Depends and leave the thinking to me!"

Willie recoiled. The words felt like a stiletto driven into his chest.

"It's our only chance," he repeated softly. "The jewelry doesn't matter. Not really."

"*Doesn't matter?* It was *mine!*" Deke whispered angrily, stabbing himself in the chest with his forefinger. "*Mine!*" He glared, eyes blazing and nostrils flaring. "I came here to take back what is mine, and I'm not leaving without it."

"None of it is really yours," Willie said softly.

"You've lost your marbles!" Deke said, gesturing dismissively, again telling Willie he was just an annoying bug. A mosquito. Worse than useless. "The cash and the drugs ain't mine, but every last piece of jewelry is. Every last piece, dammit! And I'm not leaving without it."

The sound of the shotgun being racked echoed in Willie's mind.

"You said you stole all the jewelry," Willie said. "All but this." He patted the locket holding the ashes.

"So what?" Deke sneered.

"None of the rest was ever really yours."

Eyes blazing, Deke opened his mouth to snap back a response, but stopped.

All emotion melted away from his face.

"Out of the mouths of babes," Deke finally said, shaking his head in stunned disbelief. "You're saying even if I walk away empty-handed except for that stupid locket, I'm still walking away even."

Willie wasn't sure what Deke meant about babes but nodded his head and began stuffing the cash carefully back into the safe.

"I'm counting to three!" boomed the gravelly voice above. "I better hear the clatter of guns on the floor down there."

"How do we know you won't just shoot us?" Deke called up to the unseen man.

"You don't," he said. "But it's the only shot you got."

Deke's shoulders slumped. He slowly exhaled and watched as Willie put the last of the cash back into the safe, piled neatly beside the packets of cocaine. As if they'd never been touched.

"We ain't in much of a negotiating position, are we?" Deke said to Willie.

Willie shrugged.

"Here goes nothing," Deke said, and crossed himself.

Deke bent low and sent the Glock skidding noisily along the ragged cement floor toward the base of the stairs.

"We were just trying to steal back what Rocco and Butchie stole from me a couple days ago," Deke said. "Nothing more. Tit-for-tat. Just wanted to get back"— Deke looked at Willie and shrugged—"what I thought was mine. But we failed. You win. It's all yours. We're just a couple useless old men who only want to walk away. Never bother you again. Not worth you getting a double-murder rap."

Willie patted the locket and wished for good luck.

The odds weren't great, but he thought he might make it to *nine-oh-crap*, after all.

ROLE OF A LIFETIME

S ometimes a story just drops in your lap.

Such was the case with "Role of a Lifetime." One pre-pandemic evening, my mom and I were enjoying dinner at the elegant restaurant within her retirement facility. As was typically the case, we'd been paired with two other residents, a practice designed to maximize social interactions. Mom met many new friends that way.

We conversed with the husband and wife we'd been seated with, having a wonderful time, and then, they dropped the story into my lap. Quite out of the blue, the wife mentioned another resident who... in the interest of avoiding spoilers... I'll say only that the resident behaved exactly as Edward does in this story.

A gift-wrapped story from the literary gods.

What's more, a new anthology theme had just been announced—Happy Accidents—which fit the story like a glove. What were the odds?

As it turned out, I later received yet *another* gift. Originally, I'd given the story a vastly inferior title, but Kristine

Kathryn Rusch, my co-mentor along with Dean Wesley Smith, read the story and suggested the infinitely better one you're seeing now.

With some stories, all you have to do is avoid screwing it up.

ROLE OF A LIFETIME

It was a role he'd played many times. Grieving husband. Or brother, or son, or father. In cinematic films, TV dramas, and on the stage.

And because he had always believed that to be truly great, an actor has to *become* his character—has to think like him, has to react like him, has to feel and smell and taste what the character feels and smells and tastes—Edward Huntington had willingly allowed his heart to be ripped out every time. He'd suffered the emotional wreckage as if it were his own, because he *made* it his own.

He had cried real tears. Had shaken with the agony of grief he'd felt in the deepest part of his soul, wrapping his arms around himself and holding on as if for survival. Had awakened with the sour, bitter taste of loss in the back of his throat. Had looked out onto the bleak landscape of a life torn asunder and bereft of hope, and wondered how he could carry on.

Edward Huntington hadn't wondered how his character could carry on; he had wondered how *he* could carry on. The darkest of depressions had overcome *him*. The sense of overwhelming despair had consumed *him*, had devoured *his* soul. Because he had in every way *become* his character.

Yet all of that hadn't prepared him for this.

For the real thing.

Myra was gone, his wife of fifty-seven years. His rock. Not a rock that had eroded over time, but instead one that accreted a new layer with every disappointment suffered and every triumph celebrated, each one bonding them together even more tightly.

And now she was gone. Cancer. Of course.

Leaving him alone. Childless. An eighty-one-year-old man who looked like a late-career Clint Eastwood though much shorter, only five-nine. White hair thinning on top, a weathered face—his last facelift had been two decades earlier—and a slender, almost bony frame, just a little bit stooped.

Alone in his spacious—now far too spacious—two-bedroom, sixth floor condo in the affluent Golden Sunsets retirement village an hour north of Boston. The smells of tomato sauce, shrimp cocktail, pastries, alcohol, perfumes, and cologne lingered in the air from the post-funeral reception Edward had hosted, enduring thirty-seven guests for almost two full hours, hours that had felt like days if not years.

Edward had been alone then, too, even as he forced himself to mingle. Alone, suffering the pitying looks, the words of concern, the endless well-intentioned remembrances, and the forced laughter intended to drown out a sorrow that couldn't be drowned. And when he closed the door behind the last guest, the cold blast of memories assaulted him anew.

Myra. Her rust-colored, curly hair. Bright red lipstick. A smile that began with twitches at the corners of her mouth. Her early-morning routine of sitting at the circular kitchen table reading the *Boston Globe*, sipping her steaming-hot coffee. Black, two Sweet'N Lows.

Edward faced the wall to his left. On it, Myra had hung twelve framed eight-by-ten photographs of his greatest successes, arranged in three rows of four. In each photograph, he and Myra stood beneath a marquee of a film or stage play. The oldest dated all the way back to their twenties; the most recent, almost four decades later. After every film or stage play in which he played a part of any significance, even the ones he knew were going to bomb, they'd found a marquee and got the picture taken. These were the twelve best.

Her idea.

He had called Myra his co-star, and she had swatted his elbow every time, telling him to stop being silly. But even though she'd never acted in even a single production, not even as an extra, he'd felt that way.

Co-stars. Equal billing.

He had wanted to post pictures of her successes as a professor of English literature, but she'd dismissed the idea, refusing to have her picture taken while lecturing, and saying the only thing more boring than correcting a stack of term papers was a photograph of someone correcting a stack of term papers. Myra had had no interest in the limelight, no matter how he'd tried to share it with her.

So he had just told her often, "I couldn't have done it without you."

And meant it.

Now...

Now, he doubted he could do *anything* without her. Even if, at age eighty-one, there wasn't that much left to do. Clint Eastwood could play crusty old man roles in *Gran Torino* and *The Mule* because he was Clint Eastwood. But even though the name Edward Huntington had once been a name directors thought of—at least eventually, if not as a first, second, or third choice for a significant role—it wasn't one thought of anymore.

He hadn't chosen retirement. It had chosen him.

Feeling a crushing darkness settle over him, Edward tottered unsteadily through the front room to the bedroom. The day's fading light streamed in from the bedroom's large window on his right, the beams landing on the king-sized bed, one that now promised to feel all too empty when he crawled in it. On the left, the bedroom gave way to a wide hallway to the bathroom. Myra's vanity was on the left side of the hallway, her closet on the right.

He walked to the vanity, its five-foot-wide mirror framed by white wood with ornately sculpted birds spaced every eighteen inches apart. Myra's lipstick, foundation, mascara, and other makeup rested in their chrome-colored cases on the left. Her wig, necessary after the chemo, sat on its globe-shaped holder on the right. Edward sat down on the matching white wooden bench, took one look at himself in the mirror, and quickly stumbled back to his feet.

He didn't need to see the haunted look on that face. Didn't want to see that face at all.

Lightheaded, he steadied himself on the frame of her closet. After staring at the closed white door for a time, he slid it back, and stared at the ten-foot-long row of dresses, slacks, and blouses beneath an eye-level shelf that held hats, a blonde and a brunette wig she'd almost never worn, and several dark brown boxes marked memorabilia. Shoes of every style and color hung on floor racks that ran from one end of the closet to another. Edward knew he would pull down those boxes of memorabilia sooner or later, but he couldn't bear to do so now.

What would he ever do without her?

She had died just three days ago and he'd buried her today, but already the emptiness in his life felt so overpowering his knees felt weak and his stomach churned. He tried to swallow away the bitter taste in the back of his throat. He reached out to touch a light yellow dress of Myra's that had been a favorite.

Not *the* favorite, of course, because she'd been buried in that one, a thought Edward quickly pushed from his mind. But this light yellow one with a white lace collar had been *a* favorite. His fingertips reached to stroke the collar—

A spark of static electricity shot through his fingertips.

Edward jerked his hand back in surprise, yelping at the same time. He stared at the dress, then his fingers. He laughed ruefully and shook his head.

He reached out and touched the dress again, this time without shocking effect. He stroked the collar. Remembered stroking it when Myra was wearing the dress.

"How do I look?" she would ask, and cock her head

ever so slightly as if unsure he would give her a truly honest reply.

"Like the love of my life," he'd say.

"Correct answer!" she'd say, and would smile broadly, flashing teeth of brightest white when they first were married, less so as they aged. But still the smile that lighted up his life.

Edward slipped the dress off its wooden hanger. He held the dress close to him, hugged it, then held it to his face until he could detect the slightest hint of her scent. Not her perfume and certainly not her sweat.

Just the smell of *her*. All Myra. He breathed it in, fighting back the tears and choking sobs.

He clutched the dress to his chest, and began to dance.

One, two, three... one, two, three.

It was the waltz from their wedding day all those decades ago.

"You're no Fred Astaire," Edward heard her say inside his head. Smiling.

"But you *are* Ginger Rogers," he replied.

"Good line," she said.

One, two, three... one, two, three.

Edward held the dress tighter. And felt Myra grow infinitesimally more real. More real, and closer to him. Nothing like before her death, of course. Those days were gone forever. And nothing could bring them back.

But she did feel just that little bit more real. The outlines of his memories were more distinct, the images sharper. Her throaty laughter more clear in his mind. Her scent raised from undetectable to just barely perceptible.

One, two, three... one, two, three.

Edward danced not with Myra, but with her dress. With her memory. He smiled in sweet contentment.

One, two, three... one, two, three.

When the dance was done, he wanted more.

More of Myra. As much of her as he could get. He hungered for it.

And so, for reasons he didn't understand beyond the instinct that provoked the action—

He slipped the dress over his head...

... and on over his clothes.

And felt Myra's presence grow even stronger. Much stronger. Far more intense.

Like the rush of a drug injected directly into his veins.

Edward's eyes widened. His heart pounded. He swallowed hard.

"It looked better on me," he imagined Myra to say.

"I would hope so," he replied.

"We're close to the same size," she said, "but you don't fill it out very well."

"Wrong plumbing."

And in Edward's mind, they laughed long and hard and sweet and beautifully. He closed his eyes and heard the sound of her throaty laughter. Thought of all the times they'd shared such joy.

"You aren't enjoying this *that way*, are you?" she asked when they stopped laughing. "Sexually, I mean,"

"No," he said, shocked at the thought. "Not at all."

"Because I never would have guessed that about you. It would have been okay, of course. I'd have accepted it. But I never would have guessed—"

"No, it's just... that I feel you still here."

And it was true. There was nothing sexual or even faintly sensual about it. He'd never played the role of a crossdresser, a transvestite, or a transsexual, and he wasn't playing one now. This was his first experience in a woman's dress, and he felt no thrill except...

... that it was Myra's.

And he felt he hadn't lost her, after all. Not totally. He could still cling to her now, cling more tightly to his memories. For dear life.

"You're sure you're not liking this sexually?" she asked. "It's okay to say yes."

"Not at all. Zero. Zilch."

"If I see you parading around in my bra and panties, I'll know you're lying."

"I'm not going to parade around in your bra and panties," he said, then hastily added, "unless that will make me feel even closer to you."

"You really miss me, don't you?"

THAT NIGHT, they slept together—as together as a couple can be when one half is only a memory that remains in the other's mind—in a king-sized bed that felt nowhere near as empty as Edward had previously feared. He slept soundly, except for having to get up to pee twice as was his usual, waking up more than the norm when faced with the unaccustomed need to pull up the dress before unzipping his fly. He had taken off only his shoes and socks before falling asleep, unwilling to risk removing his dress shirt, pants, and briefs beneath Myra's light yellow dress.

He heard about the dress in the morning.

"Look at my dress! Look at it!" he sensed Myra scold. "Its wrinkles have wrinkles."

Edward shrugged sheepishly. "So do I."

"Don't be a smart aleck. If you're going to wear my clothes, you have to take care of them. I can't have you ruining a whole closet full of expensive clothes."

"Okay. I'm sorry."

"I never wore a dress to bed," she said from somewhere deep in Edward's mind. "Other than a couple times when I passed out, of course. So there's no reason for you to start."

"I thought there might be something special about that one," Edward protested. "I was afraid to take it off."

"That one's no more special than all of the others in my closet. Or my pajamas or nightgowns in the dresser drawers." In his mind's eye, Edward saw the twitch at the corners of Myra's mouth as she began to grin. "The only thing special is me."

Edward could only nod for several seconds before finally managing, "Very special."

"So do me a favor and wear either my pajamas or nightgowns to bed."

"Pajamas," he said, and sensed the corners of Myra's lips turn up.

THAT DAY, he never left the condo.

A widow from down the hallway, Helen Wilson, came calling. A good-looking woman, she had more than hinted the day before at her availability to console him.

Edward didn't let her in.

"I just need to be alone," Edward told her from his side of the door. That was reasonably close to the truth since what he wanted was to be alone with Myra. Or what was left of his memories.

"Of course, of course," Helen Wilson cooed. "If you need anything, some company, someone to talk to, anything, just call."

Edward didn't call. He spent the day with Myra.

His great discovery was that when he applied her bright red lipstick, it felt like she was kissing him.

THE NEXT DAY, Helen Wilson brought a homemade chicken pot pie, and sounded quite flustered when he wouldn't open the door to take it, much less invite her in to share it with him.

"I've got three weeks worth of leftovers," Edward said, looking through the peephole. He was wearing Myra's dark maroon dress, his lips coated with bright red lipstick. "It would just go to waste."

"But I made it just for you!"

"I appreciate the thought, but I really can't take it," he said. "I'm sorry."

"We could just talk. Or have a drink."

"I really would just like to be alone."

Helen clutched the chicken pot pie with both hands and glared at the door as if she could see through it. Which, of course, she couldn't. She hadn't yet fainted at the sight of him.

Finally, with an angry shake of the head and pursed lips, she stomped off down the hall.

Edward's great discovery that day was that when he put on Myra's wig, it felt like the old days when she ran her fingers though his hair. He thought of all the times she'd done that as they kissed, and found himself puckering up his lips, covered in bright red lipstick.

"I miss you," he said. "So much!"

"I'm here, baby. I'm here."

A DAY LATER, a nurse came to check on him, perhaps prompted by an aggravated Helen Wilson, or perhaps by some automatic mechanism triggered by Golden Sunsets' safety policy following traumatic events. Edward had seen the nurse, whose name he couldn't recall, in the hallways before, making her rounds. She was a pleasant, African-American woman in her late twenties or thirties. But he had no intention of seeing her.

"I need to come in and check you out, just to be sure you're doing okay," she said cheerfully.

"I'm fine," Edward said, eyeing her warily through the peep hole. Today's ensemble was a light blue blouse and a dark blue skirt. "I just want to be alone."

"I need to see you. Please open the door. It will just take a few minutes. I promise."

"Maybe another time. Not now. I insist."

"Mr. Huntington, I really must—"

"Not now!"

"Tomorrow?"

"No, I'll call you when I'm ready."

"It doesn't work that way. This is for your own health and well-being."

"I'm perfectly fine, and I wish to be left alone," Edward said. "I don't mean to be rude, but I insist."

The nurse opened her mouth, but no words came out. She shook her head, threw her hands out, palms up, as if to say, "What am I going to do?" and walked away.

Edward breathed a sigh of relief. That had been a close call.

But all he'd done was put off the inevitable. Sooner or later, he'd have to venture into the outside world, or allow a doctor in to see him and understand why he wouldn't.

Edward knew he couldn't stay holed up inside forever. He still had plenty of leftovers, but was running out of milk and a few other essentials. Eventually, he'd either have to eat in one of the dining facilities that were part of the retirement village, go out for groceries, or have them delivered. He supposed he could require that the delivery person leave the goods by the door, and then pull them in when the coast was clear. But how long could that go on?

Sooner or later, he would have to venture outside, either without Myra's clothes and possibly lose his connection—*after hell freezes over*, he heard himself say—or... he'd have to subject himself to certain humiliation by leaving his condo while wearing Myra's clothes.

That felt like an *after hell freezes over* prospect as well.

Bur it had to be done.

Tomorrow, he told himself. Or perhaps the day after. Maybe next week.

EDWARD THOUGHT he was getting the hang of what makeup choices looked best. He certainly made for an ugly-looking Myra, but he was getting better. Sitting at the vanity, he scanned his choices.

"Am I real?" Myra asked.

Edward froze. Now there was a question. Right up there with little kids asking where babies come from.

"Or am I just a memory?" she asked.

Edward had thought he knew the answer to that question. He'd been quite certain, in fact. But not anymore.

"I don't know."

THE NEXT DAY, Edward began adding two packets of Sweet'N Low to his coffee, just like Myra always had. She had been right. Coffee really did taste better that way.

He also discovered the audio-enhancing qualities of an old pair of her diamond earrings. They were clip-ons, the only clip-ons Myra owned, a family heirloom that dated back to the days when pierced ears were not as common. They attached to his earlobes and dangled for three inches of tiny diamonds set in a white gold chain, ending with the larger, though still modest, diamond at the bottom.

Actually quite attractive.

But what really mattered was that they allowed Edward to hear Myra's voice in crystal clear clarity. Like the difference between a bedside clock radio and a top-of-the-line stereo system.

"You sound..." Edward said, astounded at the difference, "... as if you're right next to me."

"I'm right here, darling."

And she proceeded to whisper the sweetest of sweet nothings into his ear.

***

THE NEXT MORNING, Edward scolded himself for leaving the toilet seat up. It had been a pet peeve of Myra's—so he'd almost never made that mistake—but now he experienced it first-hand. Still half asleep, he sat down and fell halfway into the toilet. A disgusting way to wake up.

What the hell was wrong with him?

He also found his dirty briefs on the floor beside the bed instead of in the hamper where they belonged. He'd been tired the previous night and had just tossed them on the floor and climbed into Myra's plain white pajamas, forgetting that this was another of Myra's few pet peeves.

Looking at the bedroom this morning and seeing the dirty clothes on the floor, he had to give himself a scolding. Myra had so few things she asked for, how hard was it to do them? If he couldn't put his briefs in the hamper at night, maybe he'd have to start wearing her underwear after all.

***

TWO DAYS LATER, a mental health doctor named Dr. Esther Harris arrived at the door and wouldn't take no for an answer. Short and squat, she wore white scrubs and carried a black bag. Her dark brown hair was tied up in a bun.

"It's in your contract as a protection to you," she said, trying to sound soothing and unthreatening. But Edward knew better. A chill came over him as she continued. "You can look it up. If you won't let me in, I'll be forced to call security and they'll open your door for me. I have to be absolutely certain that you are all right."

"But—"

"There are no ifs, ands, or buts about this," Dr. Harris said. "I *am* getting inside this door, and I *am* going to evaluate your situation. We can do it the easy way, or we can do it the hard way." In a suddenly soothing tone, she said, "Make this easy on yourself, Edward."

Edward glanced down at himself. A black skirt with a white blouse. Black high heels. Rust-colored wig, red lipstick, light foundation, and the dangling diamond earrings.

If he'd known the doctor was coming, he might have opted for a pair of Myra's slacks instead of the skirt and blouse, and would definitely have held off on the earrings. But Myra had rarely worn slacks, and the one time Edward had tried a pair on, he felt almost no connection with her at all. He feared he'd almost lost Myra completely. In no time, he ditched the slacks for a dress, and never intended to make that mistake again.

But now...

"I know you stopped Nurse Anderson from getting in the other day," Dr. Harris said. "But nothing is going to stop me from getting inside this door. Another minute and I'm calling security."

She pulled out her cell phone and waved it to prove her point.

Edward tried to control his growing panic, but couldn't. He couldn't let the doctor in and see him, but he couldn't stop her either.

What could he do?

What was wrong with him? He had *known* a day like this was coming, yet he still hadn't prepared for it. It was as bad as not knowing his lines the day a film started shooting.

If the doctor got in here—*when* she got in here—what could say?

What were his lines?

"You could tell her you're preparing for a new part," Myra said. "An eighty-one-year-old drag queen. For HBO."

Edward felt his pulse miraculously slow down from a roaring gallop to an easy trot. It was the oldest trick in the book. When caught doing something embarrassing, say you're doing research. Everyone who knew him as actor, knew that he meticulously prepared for his parts. He *became* his character.

Drag queens on HBO? Eminently believable. Him *becoming* his character by wearing women's clothes, makeup, and jewelry? Quite believable, if Dr. Harris knew anything about his acting career. And if she didn't, she could Google him, for Chrissakes, and find out. She might not buy it, but as cover stories went, it wasn't half bad.

Edward touched his cold hand to the doorknob to open it.

"Of course, that would be denying what we have," Myra said. "Denying it could break the connection."

Edward froze. His eyes widened. His heart turned ice cold.

Break the connection? Lose Myra? He could never do that. Nothing would be worth that.

"I don't know," Myra, or that part of his mind he identified as Myra, said. "You can gamble. Or just tell the truth."

EDWARD AND DOCTOR HARRIS sat across from each other at the small circular kitchen table. To his left and her right were the standard kitchen appliances, a countertop, and sink, all in a row beneath an array of wooden cabinets, painted white. To his right and her left, a large window overlooked floral gardens six floors below.

"This is very unusual," Dr. Harris said. She'd attempted to hide her shock at his appearance, but initially failed before recovering. "I'm inclined to have you admitted to the state hospital for observation."

"My lawyers would sue your ass from here till kingdom come," Edward said calmly, even as his pulse throbbed and his palms felt clammy. "This is not the 1950s when people like you categorized things like...like this"—Edward pointed to himself—"as mental illnesses. I am not mentally ill."

"This isn't a simple matter of crossdressing," Dr. Harris said. "You've shut yourself off from the rest of the community, which is certainly your prerogative, but it is of concern coming so close to your wife's death."

"As you said, it's my—"

"Are you aware that you're speaking in a very feminine voice?" Dr. Harris asked.

Edward blinked. No, he hadn't realized that.

"And not just any voice. As a highly skilled actor, you can adopt any accent you choose," Dr. Harris continued. "Yet you have chosen to speak with your wife's distinct Bostonian accent. Why is that?"

Edward couldn't answer. He couldn't move. Couldn't think.

Myra whispered, "You do sound like me now."

Why was he sounding like Myra? This wasn't just a role. He wasn't simply *becoming* Myra and speaking like her for some performance.

This was more than a role. This was real life. This was his way of staying close to her. Holding onto his rock and his foundation. Holding onto her for dear life.

He wasn't *becoming* Myra in real life.

Was he?

Certainly nothing supernatural was going on. Or was it? Myra had asked him the other day if she was real, and he hadn't known how to answer her. Did real mean supernatural? It had to. Which was impossible. She *had* to be just the remnants of his memories, memories made stronger by use of her clothes, makeup, and jewelry. He didn't believe in that other hugger mugger. He'd appeared in a film once based on a Stephen King short story, and that stuff was fun, but it wasn't real.

Myra wasn't a supernatural being. She was all in his mind. And he wasn't supernaturally becoming her.

Was he?

Of course not!

And he was perfectly sane. He was simply acting bizarre

because of his love for Myra, trying to keep her as close as he could. He was as sane as the next person.

Wasn't he?

Edward suddenly wondered if he knew up from down anymore. Sane...insane. Supernatural... reality. Playing a role and *becoming* Myra... or just holding onto the last shreds of his memories.

He thought he knew. But now, it was impossible to know.

Then it struck him from out of nowhere.

"This is like *Hamlet*," Edward said.

"*What?*" Dr. Harris asked.

"You know, Shakespeare," Edward said, feeling the rush of moving onto familiar ground. The best defense is a good offense. "Ever hear of *Hamlet*? Or was that not part of your curriculum, Doctor?"

"It's been a long time, but yes, I recall a little bit. Um... 'To be or not to be. That is the question.'" Dr. Harris's eyebrows raised. "Isn't that about suicide? I'm even more concerned about you now."

"No, that's... that's not my point," Edward said, remembering too late that someone like Dr. Harris would inevitably know only that line and that line alone. "A central theme of the play asks, was Hamlet merely pretending to be insane to gain advantage over Claudius or was Hamlet in fact truly insane?"

The doctor stared back blankly.

"After all, he saw a ghost no one else saw," Edward said. "Perhaps Hamlet began pretending and the insanity became real. We don't know. Uncertainty is one of the themes of the play."

"What does that have to do with you?" Dr. Harris asked, clearly uncomfortable fighting her battle on Shakespearean turf.

"That you have no way of knowing if my behavior is merely unusual or insane."

Edward almost added that he was no longer certain himself. About his sanity, about anything. It was unknowable. But that kind of talk would get him locked up for sure. So he went with what sounded the most normal—if anything could be considered normal anymore—and the least threatening.

"I'm as sane as you are doctor," Edward said. "My bizarre-seeming actions are a threat to no one. Not to me or to you or to the other residents. The simple fact is that wearing my wife's clothing helps me hold onto what is left of her in my mind, in my heart, and in my soul. It's how I stay close to her.

"It's that innocent. And it's none of anyone else's business. You may feel that it's unknowable whether I am sane or not. I may be as great of a mystery to you as Hamlet has been to all of us for several hundred years. But you'll have to try to solve that mystery while I remain here, because this is where my wife's clothing remains, and where most of my memories with my wife were made.

"If you forcibly remove me from here and I lose those memories and those clothes and whatever magic I still feel in my soul, I will sue you for every penny you own."

Silence fell over the kitchen and lasted for what felt like an eternity.

Dr. Harris finally broke the silence. "Will you allow me

to see you here several times a week until I can be certain of your status?"

Edward considered returning to the theme of uncertainty, and how she could never be certain of his status, but just said, "Yes."

"You will cooperate during those sessions?"

"Yes." If nothing else, Edward told himself, he could at least *act* sane.

"And you'll end your seclusion? You get out of this condo at least occasionally?"

That stopped Edward. "For reasons that should be obvious," he said, "I prefer not to do that."

"For reasons that should be obvious," Dr. Harris replied, "that is a requirement."

Edward stared for a long time.

"Give me a week."

"Two days."

"Four days."

"Two."

"Three."

"This isn't a negotiation, Mr. Huntington. Two. Take it or leave it."

Edward clenched and unclenched his hands. "Okay, two."

TWO DAYS LATER, with the deadline upon him, Edward stood at his door, his heart in his throat. He wore a navy blue dress of Myra's, a pair of her sensible shoes, and the dangling jade earrings. No makeup. He wanted to feel

Myra's presence and hear her voice loud and clear, but he'd wait for the lipstick's sensation of her kissing him until he got back to the condo.

If he made it back.

"You can do this," Myra said.

Edward wasn't so sure, but he had no choice. He had to step out that door. Face the shock of his neighbors. The ridicule. It would start as barely suppressed snickers, then eventually burst into outright laughter. Perhaps a few fainting attacks. Certainly nonstop whispers behind his back.

"What a shame…" and "I've never been more shocked in my life!" and "Nobody saw it coming…"

It would be worse than the *New York Times* critic, the only critic who truly mattered, delivering the most viciously demeaning review of a Broadway show Edward was in, singling him out for particular ridicule, prompting the show to close immediately after opening night.

This would be far worse. This would be a unanimous opinion. And he would have to go on performing, facing the ridicule, night after night after night.

For the rest of his life.

Or risk losing Myra as Dr. Harris carted him away to some antiseptic laboratory where she could examine him like a rare but dangerous disease.

"You can do this," Myra said once again. And then, "We can do this."

We can do this. Yes, that felt right. He couldn't get through this alone, but with Myra by his side, they could do it together. Just like the old days when she'd helped him through all the other tough times, and he'd done the same for her.

"Break a leg," she said, and Edward smiled.

Whatever the questions were, Myra was the answer. And that meant this could be his greatest success of all. There would be no photograph of the two of them beneath a marquee, but his performance would make her proud. He would not let her down.

Edward opened the door. He stepped out onto what he thought of as the stage.

This was the role of a lifetime.

TRUTH AND LIES

INTRODUCTION TO "TRUTH AND LIES"

When I looked at the ten stories that make up this collection, I knew instantly that "Truth and Lies" had to be the grand finale. No question at all. The only negative was that I'd included it several years ago in *Hell of a Band: Twelve Fantasy Stories*.

But you know what? I had thought back then it was the perfect story to close out that collection; I'm even more convinced now it's the perfect story to close out this one.

Does that sound arrogant? My apologies if it comes off that way. That's not my intent.

Here's the thing of it. I love all my stories. They're my babies. But I succumb to that worst of all parental temptations. I pick favorites. I love some of them more than others. And yes, I also occasionally worry about the ones that aren't my favorites, worry that there might be readers out there wrinkling their nose at my lesser progeny, whispering, "That is one ugly baby!"

However, I have no such worries about this cutie with sharp teeth. It certainly helps that on the way to getting published by Mark Leslie in *Fiction River: Feel the Love*, five editors reading for their own professional anthologies all said they would buy the story. "Loved it!" they said over and over. And then the *coup de grâce* to all author doubts, "Brilliantly done."

(It occurs to me that sometimes expectations get set so high that no reader's delight can ever clear that impossibly set bar. In that case, let me whisper now deceitfully, "This story is a*wful*. One of the worst of all time. You're going to hate it." Back now to our regularly scheduled programming.)

So please forgive me for gushing far too much over this beautiful baby. Please forgive my conceit that it's the perfect choice to end this very personal collection.

But let me say it one more time, as I said in *Hell of a Band: Twelve Fantasy Stories*.

I freaking *love* this story.

And I hope that as it closes out this collection, you will, too.

love Lies. She smells of roses. Dozens of red, red roses. Roses with nothing but petals.

No thorns.

She makes a bed of them for me to lie down on. She lies down beside me, holds me to her breasts, and coos sweet nothings into my ear. She strokes my cheek with the softness of a single, delicate fingertip. If she finds a tear there, Lies wipes it away. She wraps her arms around me, and in her embrace I am all I have ever hoped to be.

She tastes like honey. Sweet. Never bitter. Her skin, soft as feathers.

She wears short skirts. High heels. On occasion, fishnet stockings. Bright red lipstick on her soft, moist lips.

It's no secret. She has a tawdry reputation.

But what do I care? I am never happier than when I am with Lies. I wish I never had to leave her.

But when Truth arrives, wearing her starched white shirt, dark blue tie, and impeccably tailored Armani suit—black with a dark blue pocket square to match the tie—and sternly clicks her black Italian shoes, my beloved Lies must flee. She cannot bear the presence of Truth.

Neither can I.

Truth pretends to be my friend, putting an arm around me, giving my shoulder a squeeze, and smiling. But it's a hard, cold smile, one with no love, joy, or merriment in it. The smile of a sadist. A smile that condemns me to despair, condemns me to my own personal Hell.

"I'm doing this for your own good," Truth says, and grins her almost perfect smile. Perfect except that with its icy coldness it appears ready to crack like a sliver of a glacier cascading into the sea. Perfect except that her bright, white teeth are just a little too sharp. Perfect except that her black eyes stare at you, unblinking, and if you dare return the stare, you are drawn into their darkness as if they have no end.

I don't believe for a minute that Truth has interrupted my time with Lies for my own good. Truth says that she will set me free, but she cares nothing for me or my freedom. She hates Lies, and when she sees the two of us together, so very happy, Truth cannot stand it.

For my own good? Hardly. Truth is a sadist, ever seeking to inflict her pain, upon the likes of me—of every-one!—and upon Lies herself, who she sends scurrying into the shadows, unable to withstand her glare. It's a lust for pain that Truth can never fully satisfy.

And so she persists, each time driving Lies away.

My oldest memory of Truth and Lies was as a short, pudgy little child. Was I four, or five, or six? It does not matter. What matters is that I believed in Lies so fully, so absolutely, and she made me so very, very happy.

She came to me then in the form of Santa Claus. Laugh all you want. Mock me if you will. But I was happy! It was Christmastime and I helped my mother decorate the tree beside the staircase, dressing it with lights and bulbs of all colors and strings of silver tinsel. I squealed with delight when together we climbed the wooden stepladder and she helped me mount the glowing angel atop the tree. For weeks the house smelled of pine and home-cooked cookies: oatmeal and raisin, chocolate chip, and sugar.

I was an only child and thus had my own upstairs bedroom, small and cramped with cheap, second-hand furniture, the wood chipped and discolored with dark blotches sprinkled across its light brown hue. But it was mine. And in that little bedroom, musty with all its little boy smells, I had a dresser against one wall, a desk against the opposite one, and my bed in the middle. And I sat at that desk and wrote my letter to Santa Claus.

Unbeknownst to me, it was really to Lies.

Dear Santa, I printed in awkwardly drawn, scrawling letters. *I have tried very hard to be good.* I went on extolling my virtues that year while explaining the reasons behind my failings, certain that Santa would find merit in the one and understand the other. I then begged that he would bring me the red Schwinn bike I coveted, the one centered on page 235 in that year's Sears catalog. I even included the page number for Santa so there would be no mistake. I watched *Captain Kangaroo* on TV—never missed a show

—and even the Captain agreed that there was no bike like a Schwinn.

I told Santa how I would use my spare baseball cards, the duplicates of bad players—worthless to me despite the intoxicating residual smell of the pink, flat stick of gum that came with each pack and even today takes me back to those cherished days—and I would do like Robby Comeau down the street and attach them to the spokes of the wheels so they would go *thwack, thwack, thwack* as I pedaled proudly down the sidewalk.

And when Christmas morning arrived, I flew down the steps so fast I almost tripped and fell, surely breaking my arm or wrist or neck, but I arrived safely at the landing, and there beside the wonderfully decorated tree was the most poorly disguised gift of all time, red and green wrapping paper around what was undoubtedly the red Schwinn bike from page 235 of the catalog.

I tore that paper off, shrieking with euphoric delight.

"Santa got my letter! Santa got my letter!" I yelled at the top of my lungs, as my parents looked on, my father's arm around my mother, and they shared my joy.

I was happy, so very happy, with what Santa—what *Lies* —had brought me.

It was pure bliss until Truth, in the form of Robby Comeau's older brother, informed me what a fool I was. It was *my parents* who had bought that bike, not Santa Claus.

There was no Santa Claus. No magical appearance from him on the night before Christmas in answer to my carefully constructed letter. Only stupid babies thought that.

A fistful of joy and all of the magic was ripped out of that red Schwinn bike.

By Truth.

Robby Comeau's older brother was right, of course. There was no Santa Claus. And I was just a stupid, little baby, who couldn't help crying at what I'd learned.

But I had been *so* delighted!

Truth hadn't been able to bear my happiness. She'd had to unmask Santa Claus—unmask *Lies*—as a fraud.

For my own good? Because it was time to *grow up*?

Already, I hated Truth.

DON'T BE A BABY, I'm sure you're thinking. It was just Santa Claus. Every kid goes through that.

I don't disagree. I never said I was unique. In fact, I say the opposite. I am everyman. I am everywoman. Only the rarest exceptions walk among us.

We are all told we are special. We are all told we can be anything we want to be. Those are some of the sweetest nothings that Lies whispers in our young, gullible ears. So intoxicating, so hypnotic.

"You're special," we hear, and Lies kisses our forehead and rumples our hair as we hear those words. Words we want to hear. Words we *must* hear, for to think anything different— *"You'll never amount to anything! You're useless!"* —would be intolerable. No, we must hear, "You can be anything!"

When I first heard those words, I decided that I wanted to be an astronaut. I dreamed of floating weightlessly in space... of looking down upon the pale blue globe we call Earth... of walking on the moon, bouncing with every step like Neil Armstrong... of maybe even living on Mars and every night cleaning its dry, red grit from my spacesuit.

I dreamed it all until in the sixth grade nearsightedness forced me to get my first set of glasses, and Truth gleefully told me—I could sense the mocking glee even as the most fraudulent sadness covered her face and heavy-lidded eyes—that astronauts must have perfect twenty-twenty vision. Not a one wore glasses.

And so my dream of becoming an astronaut came crashing down to Earth. I *couldn't* be anything I wanted to be. That lie was exposed.

But I was still special, wasn't I? Surely, that much still had to be true. I was special, but had simply been misguided in my initial choice. No, I wouldn't—couldn't—be an astronaut. I'd instead be a point guard in the NBA. And when I couldn't even make the junior high team, still short and pudgy and strikingly lacking in even the most modest athletic skills, I decided I'd become a leading actor in the movies. And after striking out with the Drama Club— "hopelessly wooden delivery" is the phrase I still recall, I decided, briefly, to become the President of the United States.

No sooner did I decide on a new "anything you want to be" choice than Truth squashed it beneath her Italian-shoed foot like a cockroach on cracked concrete, grinding the sole of the shoe over what remained of that dream long after the initial satisfying crunch.

Eventually, I fell in love with the guitar. At the age of seventeen, still short and pudgy and with a forehead dotted with acne, I fell for a Fender Stratocaster just like the one Eric Clapton used to play "Layla" while with Derek and the Dominos. And for the first time, Truth couldn't slap me down and stomp me underfoot.

I wasn't half bad and I was in love. I'd play that Fender until I got blisters on my fingers and then I kept going. I didn't play that guitar to impress others or to get girls, which was impossible because I was still distinctively unattractive.

I played it because of love. Love of music. Love of the instrument. Love of creating sounds that could maybe, some day, please-God-let-it-happen *move people*.

Soon, only the most highly trained ear could distinguish my "Layla" guitar solo from the master's. Same with "Stairway to Heaven" and "Free Bird." I learned 'em all.

God help me, I was in love.

I believed I was special. And while I might not be able to pursue the most fanciful of goals—astronaut to Mars, point guard in the NBA, the next Dustin Hoffman, or the President of the United States—I believed that now I could be whatever I wanted to be because I had found my true calling. I would be a musician, a guitarist, who would create art people would appreciate, enjoy, and remember.

This was within my reach. I was, after all, special.

And so I spent decade after decade pursuing that dream. Traveling the country. Getting ripped off by one bar owner after another. Getting ignored by one drunk after another. Living hand to mouth. Missing so many meals that I was still short but no longer pudgy. I took on the near emaciated look of the severely addicted, though I never once touched any drug.

I kept going long after every chord of common sense screamed in a cacophonous howl that I was wasting my time.

IN THE END, I wasn't special. Not at all. I was a dime a dozen. If that. Whether performing alone or part of a band. Whether the front man or back in the shadows.

In the approximate words of more than one bar owner after he stiffed me my fair due, "There are a million, billion guys like you. As soon as one of you drops dead, another ten come along to take your place. It don't matter to me. It don't matter to no one."

Believing that I was special, believing that I could be what I so desperately wanted to be—*believing Lies*—I gave my all. In the process, I forfeited all attempts at true love. I even wrote a song about it, "You're Never Home, and I Got Lonely." Not a half bad song and with a catchy guitar riff in the middle, if I may say so myself. But other than a whole lot of drunks in a whole lot of bars, hardly anyone heard it. And seems like no one remembers it at all.

No, don't get me started about true love. Don't you *dare* get me started.

And what did I end up with when it was all said and done?

I'm broke. In every which way. Financially, to be sure. I'll never pay off the hospital bills. But my body is also broken. Hands and fingers now arthritic. The ringing of tinnitus roars in my ears all day like an aural stabbing, the payday for years of turning the volume up to the max.

Nobody remembers me or my music. Whatever joy I gave those who heard me play is forgotten, and perhaps never even existed in the first place.

I wasn't special at all.

Not one bit.

"Only the very select few are special," Truth says to me in a tired tone usually reserved for speaking to simpletons. "That's what makes them special."

Over and over, she says those words, mocking the gullibility of my youth when I believed that I truly was special, and even worse, that same gullibility that continued as an adult.

I'm a fool. At last I know it.

"Acceptance is the first step," Truth says, not fully suppressing a smirk. Then she adds with that duplicitous gleam in her eye, "I'm only trying to help."

THE END IS NEAR. I've run the full gamut. I lie in my death bed, gaunt almost to the point of skeletal, my breathing agonized and wheezing, like an accordion being drawn slowly in and out. My ragged clothing is drenched in sweat, both old and new. The sheets reek of urine.

I am, of course, alone. Alone except for Truth.

Would that I be alone.

"You've wasted your life," she says. "You're going down into the ground. Worm food. Ashes to ashes. Dust to dust. Nothing more remains. Your light will be extinguished, and no one will remember."

And then finally, she leaves, whether as one final parting

mercy or far more likely, because there's no more sadistic sustenance to suck out of my marrow.

And so I call for Lies to come join me. I plead. I've never needed her more.

Lies, I beg of you, come to me now, I cry out in a death-like rasp, my mouth and lips dry. Tell me that I was special, even if I was not. Tell me that I will be remembered, even if I have already been forgotten. Tell me that I had worth even if that was no more than a dime a dozen.

I was special! I need to hear it! You can't whisper those words to me when I am young and then fall silent now!

And then I feel her presence all about me. The smell of her roses. The stroke of her feather-soft fingertips upon my cheek. Her kisses upon my ears.

Thank you! From the bottom of my heart, thank you for not abandoning me now.

I love you, Lies. I have always loved you. I have worshipped you all my life.

Lie down beside me now. Forgive the rank smells of death. I can do nothing about them.

Here. Right here. Yes.

Hold me. Forgive me for shaking.

Yes, that is good. Yes.

Now whisper into my ears those sweetest words of all. Tell me that something other than darkness awaits me. It need not be eternal bliss. Perhaps a chance to live it all over again, and next time get it right. Next time, I can be special. Or eternal bliss. That would be best of all. Of course, eternal bliss!

Anything but the darkness.

Yes, I can see the bright light coming for me.

Thank you, my sweet, sweet Lies. Thank you.

It is coming closer now. Closer and closer still.

Bless you for giving me this one last relief. Anything but the darkness.

Lies, I have always loved you. You are the sweetest and fairest of them all.

I will always remember you. Somewhere in your loving heart, Lies, please remember me. Even if you won't, please say that you will.

Thank you for your interest in my books.

D H H

NEWSLETTER

Be the first to know!

If you love my writing, my newsletter is a great way to keep up with new releases, special promotions, and other content that's only available to my newsletter subscribers.

What are you waiting for?

Sign up at www.hendricksonwriter.com/newsletter-free-story/ today!

Cape Cod Chips, Wiener Dogs, and Swiping Left: Stories of Sweet Romance (forthcoming)

The Soulmate Junkie and Other Stories of Fantasy & Science Fiction (forthcoming)

Crime From Another Time: Stories of Mystery and Suspense (forthcoming)

Crime Fantastique: Stories of Mystery and Suspense (forthcoming)

Crime, Up Close and Personal: Stories of Mystery and Suspense (forthcoming)

Nonfiction

How to Get Your Book Into Schools and Double Your Income With Volume Sales

Travis Roy: Quadriplegia and a Life of Purpose

Hendu's Story: From Dream to Reality

ACKNOWLEDGMENTS

To Kristine Kathryn Rusch, Dean Wesley Smith, Leah Cutter, and Mark Leslie, editors who believed in these stories.

To Annie Reed, editor of this collection, whose expertise I can always rely on.

To my readers, whose enthusiasm helps keep me going.

To all my family and friends, who support me during the valleys and celebrate with me on the mountaintops.

And above all, to Brenda, The Best Wife Ever, for always being there and filling life's journey with such joy.

David H. Hendrickson's first novel, *Cracking the Ice*, was praised by *Booklist* as "a gripping account of a courageous young man rising above evil." He has since published seven additional novels, including *Offside*, which has been adopted for high school student required reading.

His short fiction has appeared in *Best American Mystery Stories 2018*, *Ellery Queen's Mystery Magazine*, *Thrill Ride - the Magazine*, *Heart's Kiss*, almost every issue of *Pulphouse Fiction Magazine* and *Mystery, Crime, and Mayhem*, as well as numerous anthologies, including over a half dozen issues of *Fiction River*. He is a multi-finalist for the Derringer Award, and his story "Death in the Serengeti" was honored with the 2018 Derringer Award for Best Long Story.

He has published five short story collections with five more forthcoming. Currently available: *Shimmers and Laughs: Eight Wildly Hilarious Tales*; *Death in the Serengeti and Other Stories: Ten Tales of Crime*; *The Boy in the Boxers and Other Stories of Sweet Romance*; *Hell of a Band: Twelve Fantasy Stories*; and *Fighting the Dying Light: Stories of Aging*.

Hendrickson has published over fifteen hundred works of nonfiction, most notably his first book for writers, *How to Get Your Book into Schools and Double Your Income with*

Volume Sales, and also *Travis Roy: Quadriplegia and a Life of Purpose* and *Hendu's Story: From Dream to Reality*. He has been honored with the Joe Concannon Hockey East Media Award and the Murray Kramer Scarlet Quill Award.

Visit him online at www.hendricksonwriter.com.